"I've had it with you, Ethan King..."

"Excuse me?"

"I've tried to," Ada continued. "Believe me, I have tried to excuse you, but you don't make that very easy."

"I don't know what you're talking about, Ada."

Ethan tried to turn his attention back to the crib, but she marched closer.

"I get on your nerves, do I?"

"You are right now."

"I'm always saying things wrong?"

He stood up straighter. "Everyone knows that. In fact, I think you do it on purpose to get attention." It was beginning to dawn on him that she'd overheard his conversation with Aaron. That wasn't good.

"I'm opinionated and..." She'd been ticking items off on her fingers, but now she shook her pointer finger at him. "And I can't cook!"

"You burned a casserole that only needed heating up. How does a person do that?"

"I am so mad at you..." She stomped her foot, which caused him to smile.

He should be in a duck-and-cover position—not thinking about how beautiful Ada Yoder was when she was angry.

Vannetta Chapman has published over one hundred articles in Christian family magazines and received over two dozen awards from Romance Writers of America chapter groups. She discovered her love for the Amish while researching her grandfather's birthplace of Albion, Pennsylvania. Her first novel, *A Simple Amish Christmas*, quickly became a bestseller. Chapman lives in Texas Hill Country with her husband.

Books by Vannetta Chapman

Love Inspired

Indiana Amish Market

An Amish Proposal for Christmas
Her Amish Adversary
An Unusual Amish Winter Match

Indiana Amish Brides

A Widow's Hope
Amish Christmas Memories
A Perfect Amish Match
The Amish Christmas Matchmaker
An Unlikely Amish Match
The Amish Christmas Secret
An Amish Winter
"Stranded in the Snow"
The Baby Next Door
An Amish Baby for Christmas
The Amish Twins Next Door

Visit the Author Profile page at LoveInspired.com for more titles.

An Unusual
Amish Winter Match

Vannetta Chapman

LOVE INSPIRED
INSPIRATIONAL ROMANCE

LOVE INSPIRED®

INSPIRATIONAL ROMANCE

Recycling programs
for this product may
not exist in your area.

ISBN-13: 978-1-335-59840-0

An Unusual Amish Winter Match

Love Inspired
22 Adelaide St. West, 41st Floor
Toronto, Ontario M5H 4E3, Canada
www.LoveInspired.com

Printed in U.S.A.

To every thing there is a season,
and a time to every purpose under the heaven.
—*Ecclesiastes* 3:1

This book is dedicated to Kris Stutzman.

Chapter One

October 2

Ada Yoder pushed the popcorn cart through the crowd gathered in the auction area. She paused under the banner her *dat* had recently hung declaring the Shipshewana Outdoor Market to be "The Largest Market in the Midwest," stared up at it, and shook her head. She couldn't believe *this* was her job—selling popcorn to *Englischers* and Amish alike.

Ada had been working at the market for the past three months, since she'd been fired from her job at Howie's Ice Cream. Technically, she was a girl Friday. She'd looked that phrase up. It meant "a female assistant entrusted with a wide variety of tasks." So far, she'd been entrusted with cleaning tables in the canteen, spreading hay in the barnyard and picking up trash in the parking area. Now she was pedaling popcorn.

Somehow this job wasn't quite as exotic as *girl Friday* sounded. It seemed to her that the term "girl Monday" would make more sense. Everyone knew Mondays were back-to-work days.

She should have worked harder to keep her job at Howie's. She'd received free ice cream though the pay had been quite low. Unfortunately, her tendency to chat with customers while the line built up behind them was frowned upon. Then, when she'd accidentally added mangos to the shake machine, which had clogged the machinery and caused yellow ice cream to spurt on the walls and floor, the owner had let her go.

She sighed and nudged her popcorn cart through the crowd. Her *dat* was the owner and general manager of the market, and she didn't think he'd fire her. Though it seemed she always found some new way to lose a job.

She wouldn't think about that.

She'd focus on the positive.

It was the first Wednesday in October, and the weather outside was beautiful. A cold nip in the air had caused her to run back into the house for a sweater, nearly making them late for work. As her *dat* had driven to the market, she'd chattered on about the gold and red and purple leaves scattered about each yard they'd passed.

He'd finally stopped worrying over his to-do list and smiled at the autumn day. That had made her heart happy. It had made her day feel like a success before they'd even reached the market.

Ada loved fall. She loved all the seasons. She pushed her popcorn cart through the crowd of people gathered for the auction. She wished she was outside, but here she was in the big ol' auction barn. She would never in a dozen years expect to be trapped in a barn on a beautiful October day, but there you had it. Life was always taking unpredictable dips.

Though the large vendor section of the market had closed for the winter season, the auctions continued as usual. Miscellaneous and antique items were auctioned on Wednesday all year long, as were livestock animals. Horse auctions took place on Friday. She was guaranteed work at least two days a week in the auction area.

At that rate, she'd never make enough money for a new dress let alone the cell phone she'd been eyeing. Not that she would ever actually purchase a cell phone—they were Amish, and so the adults didn't approve of such. A girl could dream though. Just the thought of having the entire World Wide Window at her fingers brought a smile to her face. Her *dat* had a cell phone for the market, in case of emergencies. And the bishop had one in case church members needed him. Other than that, Ada didn't know any adults who had one; at least, no married adults. Married seemed synonymous with boring if you were to ask her.

She'd just turned twenty.

The thought of that threatened to send her mood spiraling back down. Twenty years old and she didn't have a serious boyfriend or a steady job. How depressing! She wouldn't focus on that though. Instead she turned her attention to the people around her. The crowd looked to be half Amish and half *Englisch*. All stood waiting for the auction to begin as the animals were lined up, awaiting their turn in the spotlight. Then there were the various employees. It was a hopping place for sure and certain.

Ethan, her *bruder*-in-law, was standing at the auction box, microphone in hand. Her *schweschder* Bethany had married Ethan's *bruder* Aaron just over a year ago. Both Aaron and Ethan were stand-up kind of guys. Ada thought that of the two, Ethan was better looking—nearly six feet, thin but strong, warm brown eyes and brown hair cut in the typical Amish style.

The problem wasn't Ethan King's looks.

The problem was his attitude.

He always struck her as terribly serious. Ada saw him at least once a week since Bethany had moved into Aaron and Ethan's farmhouse. He'd either changed over the last six months, or she'd never noticed how dour he was before. The guy was wound up tighter than one of Bethany's balls of yarn.

The crowd was good-sized, and Ada had already sold quite a bit of her popcorn.

As Ethan called for everyone's attention, Ada gave change to an *Englisch* woman who had a baby in a backpack. What would that feel like, to carry a baby around on your back all day?

She waved at the toddler then turned her cart toward the left side of the crowd when she heard the soft whimper of a puppy.

A puppy?

"We don't normally have canines in our livestock auction," Ethan was saying. "Today we're making an exception. As you can see, these seven beagle pups are healthy and young enough to train to be your next hunting dog. We'll start the bid at one hundred dollars for the lot."

They were selling puppies?

She supposed that people needed dogs, same as they needed horses or cows or pigs. But she couldn't remember that they'd ever sold dogs before. What was next? Barn kittens? She felt her irritation rise and tried to stamp it down. The pups would probably go to a *wunderbaar* home that had a lot of hunters.

She inched her popcorn cart closer to the front of the crowd to get a better look.

Pretty much all she could see in the crate Ethan was waving at was brown ears and brown tails. Then she heard a woman talking into her cell phone. Something about the woman's tone caught her attention. It wasn't boredom or irritation. It was business. The woman sounded as if she were haggling with someone over the cost of a bag of deer corn.

"Definitely young enough, and five of the seven are female. We should be able to breed them ASAP...certainly before this time next year."

Breed them?

Ada crept closer, trying to catch the name of the business on the back of the woman's clipboard. Stink. She couldn't see it. Tossing her change purse on the ground in between them, she stooped to pick it up and was just able to make out the words Backyard Breeders.

The woman raised her auction number, and Ethan pointed to her.

"We have one hundred, can I get one twenty?"

No one else seemed interested.

There were no counterbids.

Seven puppies were about to be sold for one hundred dollars. Seven puppies were about to spend their lives with Backyard Breeders…well, not if Ada had anything to do with it.

Ethan's gavel rang out and the woman dropped her auction number into her oversized bag. Still speaking into the phone, she said, "I'm about to collect the mutts and head out. See you in an hour."

Ada had to do something.

She had to stop this woman and save the pups!

Trundling her cart over to the employee break room, she pushed it inside then rushed over to the payment kiosk. The woman was pulling out her wallet. She tossed her auction number onto the counter. "I need to pay for the dogs."

James Lapp was handling payment. He was a couple years' older than Ada and super friendly. He told the woman her total, which included sales tax, and then shouted for one of the runners to bring over the crate.

Ada stood as straight and tall as possible and pushed her way forward. "You can't have them."

"Excuse me?" The woman was older, with bright pink lipstick that made her face look all the more pale.

"You can't have the dogs. I'm sorry, but there's been a mistake. They're not for sale."

"They are for sale. I just bid on them."

"Ada, what…?" James looked confused—his

eyes darting from Ada to the woman and back again.

"Excuse me, James." She tossed him her brightest smile then turned back to the woman. "It's not his fault, ma'am, or the auctioneer's. They simply didn't know that the dogs had already been purchased."

"Purchased by whom? No one else even bid."

"Me. I purchased them, directly from the owner, who was supposed to tell the auction." It wasn't a lie exactly. She would have done that if she'd known about them. If she had known they needed saving.

One of the young teenaged helpers walked up—he'd placed the crate on the back of a wagon and was supposed to help transfer them to the woman's car. Except these pups weren't going with this woman. No way. Uh-uh. Suddenly it seemed to Ada that the most important thing she'd ever done was to save these puppies.

"Here they are. I can hardly wait to get you home." Ada knelt by the crate, putting her fingers through the wire mesh. Immediately three of the pups began pushing up against her hand and licking her fingers. Oh, but they were so precious. To think that they might have gone with this awful woman—who was still arguing with James.

Ada stood again and faced the woman directly.

"These dogs will not be going with you. Backyard Breeders? Please. You're a puppy mill."

"You don't know what you're talking about, and since when does an auction house decide who can and can't bid on a lot?"

"It's not a *lot*. It's puppies, and I heard you on the phone…planning on breeding them ASAP. Isn't that the word you used? As soon as possible? They are puppies. You should be ashamed of yourself."

The woman's expression lost all pretense of friendliness.

"How dare you?"

"How dare I?"

James Lapp was still standing behind the payout booth, shifting from foot to foot, apparently unsure what to do.

"Let me see your cell phone, James."

"What?"

"Just let me see it. I'll give it right back."

She quickly thumbed "Backyard Breeders Indiana" into the internet search browser. What came up was a Yelp page featuring the woman's business. One glance confirmed that it contained terrible reviews and warnings in all caps.

"See?" She turned the screen toward the woman. "Puppy mill. You're not getting our dogs, and you're not welcome here."

"Fine." The woman looked more irritated than

offended. She certainly didn't deny the allegation. Instead, she stuffed her wallet back into her purse and stormed out of the auction house.

Ada felt a flush of triumph. She'd done it. She'd saved a litter of beagle puppies.

"Uh-oh," James said.

"Uh-oh? She's gone. We did it. We saved the pups!" She handed the cell phone back to James then turned to see what he was looking at with such worry.

Oh.

Ethan King was headed their way, and he did not look happy.

Ethan had passed the auction microphone over to Samuel Mast, another of the auctioneers. Something problematic was happening at the payment booth. They couldn't afford to get backed up. He'd spent quite a bit of time reading up on auctions before applying for his job. Auctions that ran quickly and smoothly brought in twenty percent more revenue.

He rushed over to the booth, working to keep his voice low so other paying customers wouldn't hear. As he approached, he notice that James Lapp looked a bit lost, or maybe embarrassed. Ada, on the other hand, had the usual blissful expression on her face as she crouched in front of the crate filled with beagle pups.

"Why did that woman leave without the dogs?"

"Because she can't have them." Ada stood and wiped her hands against the white apron covering her dark green dress. If anything, her smile had grown even broader.

"I don't understand."

"I told her she couldn't have them. She was a puppy breeder, Ethan. We couldn't let these dogs go with her."

His confusion melted into a red-hot anger. He feared his hat might blow off the top of his head or that steam would leak out of his ears. His right temple began to pulse with his increased blood pressure.

His *bruder* had been married to Bethany Yoder for a year, and he'd spent enough time with the Yoder family to know that they all spoiled Ada, who was the youngest of the five girls. She was immature, scatter-brained and irresponsible. Since he'd moved home to Shipshe, she'd gone through at least half a dozen jobs. She was also uncommonly pretty, but that had nothing to do with their current problem.

"You don't have to look at me as if I've done something terrible. I helped you."

"Ada, she bid on the lot. We can't deny her—"

"Of course, we can."

"We agreed to sell those dogs."

"The litter came from Evan Schmucker, right? Evan wouldn't want them to go to a puppy mill."

"Evan needs the hundred dollars to buy feed for his horses. Farmers are hurting this year and—"

"Oh, he'll find some other way." Ada smiled at him brightly, then a frown slowly formed between her eyes as she seemed to finally realize that he was quite upset. "Why are you making a big deal of this? It's not as if the world is beginning."

"I think you mean *as if the world is ending*," James corrected her.

Ethan shot James a stay-out-of-it look. The last thing they needed was to be distracted by Ada's ridiculous sayings.

"Ada, I have to go help with this auction."

"Fine."

"When I'm done, we are going to finish talking about this."

"Super fine."

He wondered if he should attempt to auction the dogs again, but that might send the wrong message to the crowd. As it was, few people would be aware of what had happened. He didn't want rumors to start flying about his auction being conducted in a haphazard way. He needed this job! And he needed the commission from every sale, even the one-hundred-dollar puppy sale.

"I'll just be around, pushing my cart and selling popcorn, if you need me."

She acted like this was some big joke. Did she take anything seriously? He doubted it. The world was one big playground for Ada Yoder and, at the moment, that playground included a crate full of puppies.

She wasn't going to listen to him, that much was obvious. Ethan glanced at his watch then back toward the auction stand. "It would probably be best for you and me to see Amos as soon as the auction is finished."

Ada rolled her eyes. "He's the general manager, sure, but he's also my *dat*. And he loves animals. I guarantee you that he'll take my side on this."

Coming from anyone else, the words would have sounded bratty, but Ada was simply speaking the truth. Still, they were running a business, and Amos Yoder was no fool. He understood how important the reputation of the auction was. Ada, he was certain, was about to be in for a surprise.

Two hours later, they were sitting in Amos's office.

If anything, Ada seemed more oblivious than usual.

Ethan related what had happened and then summed up his concerns about the morning's events. "I'm worried this could lead to a bad reputation for the auction. Once a lot is sold, we can't just take it back."

Amos nodded as if what Ethan had said made perfect sense. He was fifty-eight years old, his beard generously peppered with gray, and he wore wire-rimmed glasses. Though Ethan had only worked for him a month, he could already tell that he was a *gut* boss. He cared about his employees and about his business. Ethan was sure that Amos would see this situation his way.

But to his surprise, instead of agreeing with him, Amos turned to his *doschder*. Peering over his glasses, he said, "I suppose you have a different version of what happened."

"Not exactly." Her eyebrows shot up and she broke into a smile.

It irritated Ethan how young and fresh and innocent she looked. Her blond hair escaped playfully from her *kapp*, as if she'd just stopped in after a game of volleyball. The toes of her right foot tapped a rhythm on the floor. Her blue eyes sparkled. She was a slim, small thing, which made the amount of trouble she caused all the more puzzling. Ada Yoder was a child wrapped in a woman's body. She irked him; plain and simply irked him.

He wasn't sure why he had that response to Ada. Maybe it was because he'd had to become a man at a very young age, and it seemed to him that Ada still acted like a *youngie*. Now she cleared her throat and smiled at them both, finally focusing on her *dat*.

"What Ethan said is all true. The woman won the bid fair and square. In fact, I don't think anyone else even countered her bid." She glanced at Ethan for verification.

He shrugged. "True, but beside the point."

"I wasn't eavesdropping when I heard her place the phone call, but I did hear her. She didn't bother to lower her voice. Then she started talking about how many of the pups were female—five—and how soon they could breed them—ASAP."

Ada shook her head in mock disgust. Only it was probably genuine disgust because everything Ada expressed seemed to be genuine. The girl had no filter at all and she felt everything with grand gestures and pulsing emotion.

"I happened to drop my coin bag on the ground." She leaned forward and dropped her voice conspiratorially. "Actually, I threw it on the ground so I could get a look at the back of her clipboard. It said, right there in big letters, Backyard Breeders, as if she were proud of it. That's when I knew I had to intervene, so I did."

She leaned back, her version of events told.

Amos didn't speak right away, which worried

Ethan. Was he actually considering approving of what Ada had done?

"I admire your passion for the pups, Ada."

"Danki."

"Though it comes as a surprise since you often forget to feed our own dog, Gizmo."

"Oh, someone is always tossing that dog food, trust me. Have you noticed how he waddles when he walks?"

"Still, this is a side of you I haven't seen before." Amos studied her another moment. "Maybe I should put you in the auction house on a more permanent basis."

"What?" The word popped out of Ethan's mouth with more force than he'd intended.

"Hear me out." Amos raised a hand, patted the air, then continued. "For many years, *Englischers* have thought there was an Amish puppy mill around every corner, and I will admit... there were some even here in our community who treated dogs poorly."

"There are?" Ada's face creased in concern.

"Were—there aren't anymore, not with Ezekiel as our bishop. He wouldn't allow such from one of his church members. All creatures are created by *Gotte* and deserve care and respect."

"I wish you had been there to speak to this *Englisch* woman—she seemed completely unfazed by what I said."

Ethan felt they were getting off topic, but it didn't seem like the right moment to redirect the conversation.

Amos had taken off his glasses and was polishing them with a cloth he pulled from his desk drawer. "Both Amish and *Englisch* can sin, yes? And treating *Gotte*'s animals with disrespect—any of his animals—well, that would be wrong. I'm proud of you for standing up and doing what you thought was right. We don't want to be affiliated, in any way, with a company that brings harm to the animals we help to find new homes."

Ethan sank back against his chair, defeated. He couldn't believe this was happening. He didn't know what to say. He didn't even know where to begin.

Amos wasn't done though. "Despite your sudden passion for animal welfare, Ethan also has a point. Revoking on a sale isn't the kind of reputation we want."

"Danki," Ethan said softly.

Ada simply pooched out her bottom lip.

"Also, there's the matter of the money—Evan Schmucker trusted us to sell his animals. You'll need to give James Lapp a hundred dollars. He'll see that it's passed along to Evan."

"But…that's practically all the money I have."

"You should have thought of that before you preempted the sale. Evan will receive eighty-five dollars and Ethan here deserves his fifteen percent commission. Neither Evan nor Ethan should be made to pay for your sudden emboldened conscience."

"But, *Dat*..."

"In addition, it will be up to you to care for the animals until you find an appropriate home for them."

"Care for them?"

"Purchase food, see to their veterinary care, et cetera."

"Et cetera? What else is there?"

"You'll figure it out." He smiled, donned his glasses and drummed his fingertips on the top of his desk. "Now, if that's all, I have work to get back to."

"Um, Mr. Yoder..."

"Call me Amos. We're family, Ethan."

"*Ya*. Amos, you said you were going to assign Ada to the auction permanently. What exactly did you mean by that?"

"Well, it seems to me that we could use some good publicity in the animal department. She can be in charge of looking over the lots on Tuesday, letting the auctioneer know any concerns she might have, and making sure all is on the up-and-up."

"Up-and-up..." Ada seemed a bit dazed by the thought.

Possibly, she was realizing the repercussions of her actions. Ethan certainly hoped she was. He wanted to dance a jig that her oblivious smile had disappeared, but he was also more than a little worried about having Ada in his department. Look at how much trouble she'd caused selling popcorn. Now she was going to look over the lots?

They walked down the stairs and out the door of the main office building.

Ethan wasn't looking forward to working more closely with Ada, but given her reputation for losing jobs, he didn't think it was something that he would be dealing with for very long. With any luck at all, she'd get herself fired...or quit. Yes, that was the ticket. Maybe she'd grow bored and quit. He didn't wish her ill. He simply wished her to be somewhere else. Ada Yoder was not a problem he felt equipped to handle.

Chapter Two

Ada held her tongue until they'd stepped out into the noonday sunshine. She was grateful for the sweater she wore. The wind was cold, reminding her that winter was coming. She'd worry about that tomorrow. Today, she needed to straighten out the man standing beside her.

"Why don't you like me?"

He stopped midstride, turned and studied her. Twice he started to speak, but each time he stopped himself. His face had colored too. She seemed to have hit that board on the head.

"I can't believe it. Everyone likes me. I'm very likable. You are a hard mirror to crack, Ethan King."

"I think you mean hard nut to crack."

"And I guess I know what I mean. I've cracked a mirror more than once and let me tell you it's a mess to clean up. Do you dislike women in general or just me?"

"Ada, I don't dislike you."

"Now you're being untruthful." She walked across the sidewalk to a bench and flopped onto it. Life was exhausting sometimes. People were exhausting. "I can't fathom a single thing I've done to offend you."

"Ada, you interrupted an auction. You basically took money out of my pocket."

"So?"

"So?" His eyebrows arched and he put his hands on his hips as if he were a teacher about to deliver a lecture.

Ugh. Ada had not liked school or those lectures she'd received all too often. "It's only money, Ethan. It's not life."

"But, for some of us, money makes life possible." He looked as if he wanted to storm off, but instead he sat beside her. Not too close though. He left a good foot of space between them. "Do you remember when I said that Evan needed the money from the sale of the beagles? That he needed to buy feed for his horses?"

"I remember."

"And do you realize that the spring brought floods followed by a summer with record-low rains?"

"Oh, *ya*. I know there wasn't enough rain. I was supposed to go kayaking in Bristol last

August. Have you been, Ethan? The St. Joseph River is beautiful, but…"

She'd been terribly upset that they couldn't go. She'd looked forward to that day for months. Thinking of it now, she wondered why life was like that—so full of ups and downs. At least there were the ups though, which is what she preferred to focus on. Unlike the man sitting beside her.

"We weren't able to go kayaking because the water level was too low. It was a real disappointment."

"That must have been hard on you," he said sarcastically.

"Oh, it was. We had to go to the park instead, which wasn't nearly as much fun."

Ethan sat forward, elbows on his knees, palms pressed together as if he were praying for patience. Was he praying for patience? What had she done now?

"Ada, I want you to listen carefully."

She turned her attention to him. Ethan was always so sad and so serious. Maybe it was because of his parents. His *dat* had a terrible disease that made him very energetic then desperately despondent. His *mamm* and *dat* had finally moved to Sarasota so that Ethan's grandparents could help with his *dat*'s care. Ethan and Aaron had been given the family farm and were trying to make a go of it. She thought he'd be a lot more successful if he'd simply improve his attitude a little.

"Most of us lost our crops this year. I know I did." He ran the thumb of his right hand over a callus on the palm of his left. "It's why I'm working here at the auction. My barn's roof needs fixing, and I'd like to add on a room for Bethany and Aaron's *boppli*."

Her mood brightened suddenly at the mention of her pregnant *schweschder*. "I am so excited about that—Bethany and Becca pregnant at the same time. Just think, our family will welcome two *bopplin* in the same month. It's going to be quite a Christmas."

"Don't you want what's best for them?"

"Of course."

"You're certain?"

"I'm offended that you would even ask."

"It costs money to build the room. Money I would have made from the crops, but now I'm working here. That's why every sale is so important. That's why every commission matters."

She shook her head in disbelief. "You need the faith of a tomato seed. That's what you're missing."

"Mustard seed."

"Have you ever seen a mustard seed? I'll bet not, but you've surely seen a tomato seed—everyone has. Anyway, have a little faith, Ethan. The *bopplin* will be fine." She stood, straightened her dress and apron and sweater, then ducked her head and wagged a finger at him.

"You need to lighten up. Now, if you don't mind, I need to go and pick up my puppies."

He sighed so heavily that she could hear the air whoosh out of him. "I need to head back that way too. I'll walk with you."

They were quiet as they made their way toward the auction barn. Ada stopped outside the door and stared up at the structure. "I have a new job."

"Girl Friday didn't last very long."

"I don't mind that. When *Dat* first suggested it, I thought he meant I'd only work on Fridays. I was certainly disappointed to learn it meant something else entirely—cleaning the barnyard and pushing the popcorn cart." She shivered, grateful that she'd narrowly missed being stuck in that job all winter.

Then she glanced at Ethan, wondering if she'd managed to brighten his outlook any. She often thought that was her mission in life—to help other people find a brighter outlook.

Ethan didn't laugh, not exactly, but a smile tugged at the corner of his mouth. He was indeed a hard mirror to crack, but Ada thought that perhaps she'd made a little progress.

"We're going to be working together, Ethan... every week."

"Indeed."

"If you could be a little less serious..."

"And if you could be a little more so..."

She turned on him, extended her hand, and lowered her voice. "I'll try, but no crying over spilled juice, okay? The puppy thing is behind us. Going forward, we'll make a great team."

He shook her hand, quickly dropped it and rushed off in the opposite direction.

This guy. He was something else—something she didn't understand at all. Did he act so stand-offish around all women, or only around her? She wasn't sure which would be worse.

Some people remained a puzzle to her.

But she did have a new job, and it sounded like more fun than selling popcorn. Maybe it was *the* job—the one she'd be *gut* at, the one she'd keep for a long time. Ada wanted to love work the way her *schweschdern* did. Sarah loved keeping the family home in tick-tock shape. Becca's favorite thing in the world was to work on a mission job. Eunice loved creating new gadgets, and Bethany loved knitting. Everyone in her family had found their calling. Everyone except her.

What if she didn't have one?

What if there was no reason for her to...be?

At least now she had something that needed her—seven little beagle puppies.

As for that new dress or cell phone, it didn't look like she'd be purchasing either of those anytime soon. On the other hand, as she'd told Ethan, *It's only money...it's not life.* She believed that, too, and honestly, she didn't really care about the phone. But the dress? She would have looked nice in a new dress. It was a pity that instead of fabric she'd be purchasing dog food.

Ethan helped close out the day's auction—which involved making sure every buyer had the merchandise they had paid for, every receipt was in the logbook, and the funds received had been deposited at the bank. By the time he was done, the sun was setting. Ada and her puppies were long gone. At least he wouldn't have to walk to the parking area with her. He had no idea what to say to women in general, and Ada in particular.

She was so open, honest, and trusting. Normally he found those to be admirable qualities, but in Ada they seemed to scratch up against his soul. She didn't take anything seriously enough, not even the birth of two children into their family. Ethan, on the other hand, was determined that his new niece or nephew would not suffer as he had. Nope. This child that Aaron and Bethany were having would never hide from their father in the barn, or worry if there was enough food on the table, or wear clothes that no longer fit.

All things that Ada Yoder couldn't even conceive.

He shook his head as he climbed up into his buggy and called out to Misty, their old mare. Back in the spring—when the crops had looked as if they'd come in well, back before the weeks of rain that had flooded the fields—he and Aaron and Bethany had purchased another mare.

Dixie was solid black and eight years old. He'd rather have purchased a younger mare—one they could count on lasting twenty years. But Dixie had been a good compromise and much less expensive. They'd also purchased a used buggy.

Of course, he'd insisted that Aaron and Bethany take the younger horse and newer buggy—although it wasn't brand-new, it did at least have a heater in it. The buggy he drove had no heat at all. In fact, it was the same buggy that his parents had bought when they were first married. What with his *dat*'s bipolar disease, there had never been money to upgrade things.

He didn't mind driving the older buggy or the older mare.

Misty was now twenty-one years old. She often fell asleep if she was left waiting for any amount of time at all. Still, she was a *gut* and faithful horse.

What would they do when Misty could no longer pull a buggy? With the failing crop, they couldn't afford to purchase another horse, or fix the barn, or add on the room for the new *boppli*. The lack of funds frustrated him, especially since it felt as if he worked all the time.

He didn't mind working.

But he wanted to be able to provide for his family—even for his *bruder*'s family.

It's only money...it's not life.

Ada's words rankled him.

It was something that a person who always had plenty of money would say. What did she know about budgeting and not having enough? Sure, he'd heard the stories that Amos had struggled when he was a young widower with five girls to raise. He'd started out as an auctioneer at the market that he now owned and managed. Amos did not have to worry about money. He was a generous man, and he would have given Aaron and Ethan whatever they'd needed, but Ethan wasn't ready to ask for that.

He and his *bruder* were men now. They were adults. They should be able to make their way.

It's only money...it's not life.

Ada reminded him of a newborn doe. She was trusting and innocent and clueless. Yeah, definitely clueless.

How could someone so beautiful be so infuriating?

He turned Misty onto Huckleberry Lane, unable to remember one moment of the drive home. He'd been oblivious to the stunning fall colors and the beautiful Indiana countryside. After unharnessing Misty and putting her in her stall along with a bucket of oats, he hurried toward the house. Bethany always had dinner on the table at six o'clock sharp.

The smell of baked chicken wafted toward him as he walked into the kitchen.

"I was hoping you'd make it in time to eat with us." Bethany turned and gave him a genuine smile.

Ethan had never had a *schweschder*, but he was finding that he liked it. Bethany had just entered the third trimester of her pregnancy, and her stomach protruded in front of her in a way that made Ethan worry she might topple over. He couldn't imagine her getting even bigger. He knew next to nothing about pregnant women and *bopplin*.

It worried him that they might do something wrong.

Should Bethany be standing in the kitchen and cooking? Yet he knew that many Amish women did work right up until they gave birth. He simply didn't know what was normal, what wasn't, and what should change.

Aaron, on the other hand, had settled into the role of husband and expectant *dat* like a duck took to water. He walked into the room, slapped his *bruder* on the back and asked how the auction had gone.

"*Gut*, other than a run-in with Ada."

Bethany, Aaron and Ethan each grabbed a dish and set it on the table—baked chicken, potato casserole, baked squash, fresh bread and a salad. They might not have a *gut* roof on the barn yet, but they ate like royalty.

Once they'd silently prayed, Bethany passed him the chicken. "What has my little *schweschder* done now?"

He told them about the debacle with the puppies. Like many things in life, it was funnier in the telling than the actual event had been. By the time he got to the part where Ada accused the woman of running a puppy mill and the woman stormed off, Bethany was staring at him—eyes wide, and Aaron was smiling down at his plate.

Waiting until he was sure that Ethan was done, Aaron snagged another piece of bread. As he buttered it, he observed, "She's a hoot, Ada is."

"She's rather a mess—no offense, Bethany."

"Oh, I agree. We all know that about Ada, but we love her even more because of it."

"*Ya*. I get that, but—"

"She has no memory of *Mamm*, you know. Neither do I, not really. Sometimes I think I remember some detail, but then I realize it's something that Sarah or Becca told me. Eunice might remember a little—she was four when *Mamm* passed. I was two and Ada was one."

"I'm sure that was difficult." He'd heard this story several times before, and he did feel sympathy for the girls. They weren't the first to lose a parent though. It wasn't an excuse for refusing to face the realities of life. "Still, Ada will have to grow up at some point."

Bethany cocked her head, one hand holding her fork, the other resting on the side of her stomach. "Wouldn't it be *wunderbaar* if she could keep her attitude and cheerfulness though? I think we could all use a little more of that."

Aaron met Ethan's eyes and shook his head once, definitively. He didn't want Ethan to argue with his *fraa*. He didn't want to upset her in any way, and Ethan understood that.

Later, when they were in the barn completing the evening chores, they picked up the conversation.

"What's really bothering you about Ada?"

"I'm not looking forward to her checking my animals before the auctions take place."

"Why? What's the worst that you can imagine happening?"

"Let's see." Ethan leaned the pitchfork he'd been using to clean Misty's hay against the stall door and began ticking off possible nightmare scenarios. "She could insist that all chickens be free range…"

"Most Amish chickens are free range."

"She could argue for better living conditions for cows."

"Our cows seem pretty content to me."

"Then there's the concerns about pig rights…"

Aaron was smiling now. "You're kidding. Right? Do you think Ada has become an animal rights' activist? Those sorts of people might be necessary in the *Englisch* world where there are huge cattle or chicken operations, but Amish own small farms. Amish children feed the chickens, let them loose every day. Amish cows are often treated like the family pet."

"I don't know what Ada has become. Things catch her attention for a moment and then they're gone."

"Which is why you shouldn't worry."

"If you could have seen her with those puppies. It was like she'd finally found her life's calling."

Aaron closed Dixie's stall. When she stuck her

big head over the half door, he offered the horse a peppermint. Ethan did the same for Misty.

"Have you ever thought about why you get along so well with Bethany's other *schweschdern*, but not Ada?"

"It's not a mystery. Sarah's responsible and pleasant. Eunice has an amazing brain and work ethic. Becca and Gideon went on another mission trip last summer—you have to respect that. And Bethany, well, she's been the best *schweschder*-in-law I could hope for."

"So you like the family I married into."

"I do."

"You approve."

"Of course, I approve." The question annoyed Ethan. It wasn't up to him to approve or disapprove of Aaron's choices. On the other hand, when living on a small farm or in a small community, each person's choices tended to affect the rest of the family.

"Then explain your problem with Ada."

"Honestly, I can't. I try not to let her get under my skin but then something like today's events happen…"

"Fifteen dollars isn't such a big deal."

"Fifteen dollars is fifteen dollars. You know that we need every cent we can make. Our plan depends on—"

Aaron held up a hand. "I'm aware of our plan

to make this farm profitable, but not everything goes as planned. You know that."

Ethan sighed, but he didn't answer.

"Not everything is under your control, *bruder*. Maybe you should just relax a little and trust *Gotte*."

That sounded too much like Ada's advice for Ethan's taste. It also sounded like what Ethan had said to Aaron the year before when he was afraid to admit his feelings for Bethany. Somehow, somewhere along the way, they'd swapped positions.

"It could be that you're attracted to her."

"What?" The denial came out stronger than he'd intended, but good grief—what was Aaron thinking?

"She's *gut*-looking."

"That she is."

"You already know and like the family."

"Just stop."

"And now you're going to be working directly with her."

"Something I am *not* looking forward to."

Aaron grinned. "I'm just saying…maybe it's because you like her. You see how happy Bethany and I are, and you want the same. That's natural enough."

"You are reading this all wrong."

"Okay. If you say so." Aaron's expression conveyed that he obviously thought he was on to something.

"I'll give you the fact that she's the prettiest of the Yoder girls."

"You mean after Bethany."

Ethan waved that away. "Her misquotes make me crazy."

"See? You need to lighten up."

"And she's so…immature for her age."

"I guess." They closed up the barn and walked toward the house. "Maturity can be overrated though. I wish our *mamm* could have been a little more lighthearted. She always seemed so sad and pushed down by life's problems."

It was true. The burden of their *dat*'s illness had weighed heavily on their *mamm*.

"Ethan…" Aaron waited until Ethan had turned back toward him, had turned his attention completely toward him. "I appreciate your worrying about things around here—the barn roof and an extra room for the *boppli*…"

"Of course I worry about things. We're a family. We take care of each other."

"True, but it seems to me that those things you're worried about aren't strictly necessary. The barn's roof will hold with the patches for another year, and the *boppli* can sleep in our room. It's not a hardship."

Ethan nodded because he knew that's what

Aaron needed him to do. "Think I'll sit out on the porch awhile."

"Suit yourself. Work wore me out today. I'm headed inside."

Aaron and Bethany managed the market's RV park. Though it had been lightly used when first opened, the Plain & Simple RV Resort was usually full now. Even in the midst of winter, they sometimes had a waiting list. Aaron enjoyed the work, as did Bethany, though her days there were definitely numbered.

Ethan sank into the old rocker on the front porch and stared out at the stars. His mind raked back over the conversation with his *bruder*. He felt as if he hadn't explained himself well. In truth, he didn't really understand his irritation toward Ada.

It wasn't attraction though.

He'd been attracted to women before and, yes, he hoped to marry one day. When he did, it would be to someone like him—someone mature and responsible.

As for Ada, *Gotte* help the man who fell in love with her.

Chapter Three

Ada could tell that Sarah was worried. Her elder *schweschder* had that concerned look that caused a wrinkle to form between her eyes.

"I'll be fine. You know I've always liked animals."

"I do not know that."

"Well, maybe it's something I'm only beginning to realize. It could be I'm a late grower."

"Bloomer?"

Ada shrugged. They were in the kitchen, cleaning up the breakfast dishes. Her *dat* had left early in one buggy. Ada would be riding with Gideon in the other buggy. Becca would be staying home.

"Just because I'm in my seventh month doesn't mean that I want to sit around all day eating bonbons." Becca walked into the kitchen, pulling on her dress. "Though the way I'm gaining weight, you would think I do eat bonbons all day."

"You're supposed to gain weight when you're pregnant, and I'm sure that you'll be plenty busy here at home." Gideon squeezed her hand and kissed her cheek. "There's nothing to do at the market anyway. No vendors at all—only preparing for tomorrow's livestock auction."

Becca snapped her fingers. "That's what I could do. I could start preparing for our Christmas market."

Everyone in the kitchen groaned, and Gideon escaped through the mudroom to ready the buggy.

Becca's favorite time of year was Christmas, and her enthusiasm for the sacred holiday sometimes drove those around her to distraction.

Sarah, Eunice and Ada turned to face Becca. All three were standing at the kitchen sink. All three stood with their backs against the counter and their arms crossed.

"Please remember it's only October," Sarah said.

"This will be our third year to hold the Christmas market," Eunice added. "I'm not sure how we could improve it more than we already have. Though I have been thinking about using solar panels to create a light display in the parking area."

"We have electricity at the market." Ada wriggled her nose. "Why do we need solar panels?"

"Because we're keeping it…"

"Plain and simple," the four *schweschdern* said in unison.

Ada voiced what everyone was thinking. "Gosh, it's times like this that I miss Bethany."

"She's a fifteen-minute buggy ride away." Sarah turned her attention back to the skillet she had been scrubbing.

"I might end up spending the day letting out my dresses." Becca sank into one of the kitchen chairs. "This one's too tight, same as the others."

"It was on my list of things to do." Sarah set the pan in the drainer and peeked out the window, then nodded toward the waiting buggy. "Ada, your chariot awaits."

"Oops. Gideon is ready to go. I better get skipping."

"Hopping," Eunice murmured.

"Let me walk you out." Sarah hooked an arm through Ada's.

"Why would you do that?" Ada nudged her shoulder against her *schweschder*'s. Sarah was the mother she'd never had, and Ada didn't know what she'd do without her.

"I just wanted to talk to you about today."

"Oh."

They stood on the porch. Gideon hopped out of the buggy and began rummaging around in the supply box welded on the back.

"*Dat*'s quite excited that you've taken an interest in the animals."

"*Ya.* I hope I don't disappoint him."

"You'll do fine."

"Then what did you want to talk to me about?"

Sarah's eyes crinkled in concern. "You do understand where the meat on our table comes from."

"Of course."

"Animals are sold at auction for two reasons—to breed or to raise as food."

"Some are sold for other reasons—some goats are raised for their milk, and some sheep are raised for their wool."

"Yes, that's true, but those cases are the exception not the norm."

"Okay."

Gideon had climbed back into the buggy and looked ready to go.

"Was that it? Was that what you wanted to talk to me about?"

"Just…try not to be emotional about things."

"Huh. Okay."

"And don't irritate Ethan."

"I've been thinking about that, and I have a plan. I won't cry over broken eggs, and I'll be nice to Ethan." Ada needed to wipe that look of concern off Sarah's face. But how? It was plain that Sarah was worried about her. Then she remembered the beagle pups in the barn stall.

"The pups are adorable. We've only had them six days, and already they seem to have grown."

She'd risen early each day to feed them, changed their water, cleaned up any soiled hay and played with them. Who knew that a litter of puppies could be so much work? It had been worth it, though, as one after another had climbed onto her lap and fallen asleep. She'd rather have spent the day there—in the barn—than at the auction.

Sarah continued to peer at her in a concerned way.

"Promise to look in on them?"

"I will."

"Everything's coming up radishes. Try not to worry so." Ada kissed Sarah's cheek and jogged to the buggy.

She talked with Gideon about Christmas plans, Becca and the baby, Bethany and her baby, and the fine fall colors. Gideon was easy to talk to. She hadn't realized that she'd wanted a *bruder* until Becca had married Gideon. Then Bethany had married Aaron. Now she had two *bruders*—three if she threw in Ethan for the fun of it. She wondered how she had managed without one all of those years.

Forty minutes later, she was walking through the livestock barn. She'd snagged a small spiral notebook out of the supply closet and paused at each animal pen to note the seller and jot down a few questions. Only about one-third of the people who were auctioning animals were there since it was the day before the sale of their lots. Many arrived early the morning of the auction rather than the day before. She couldn't imagine being at work before sunup, but she supposed she might sometimes need to be if she was going to do her job correctly.

She spied Benjamin Mast standing with a group of men. Should she wait for him to finish what he was doing or should she interrupt him? Realizing that the early bird gets the best view, she headed over to where they were standing.

The men stopped talking as soon as she approached them. Each nodded her way and two said, "Morning, Ada."

"Benjamin, I was wondering if I could talk with you a moment?"

He looked surprised, but he smiled and said, "Sure. What about?"

"Your goats."

"Okay. Let's head over to see them." He studied his herd of goats as they stopped next to the pen. "Do you know anything about goats?"

"A little. These are Boer goats, correct?"

"They are."

"And you'll be selling them for meat?"

Benjamin took off his hat, scratched his head, then replaced the hat. "Correct. Boer goats are a good breed for that since they reach maturity in ninety days."

"They're babies?" Ada almost dropped her pad of paper. Her heart thudded in her chest and her thoughts flew off in a thousand directions.

Baby goats?

Being sold for someone's dinner plate?

Suddenly she remembered her promise to Sarah and worked to bring her emotions under control. "What I mean is that they look older."

"Does can reach 200 to 230 pounds. Bucks can grow as big as 300 pounds."

The goats all had brown heads and white bodies. The smallest one was curled up on the ground, eyes wide as it watched the activity around it. Ada hated to think of any of them being on someone's dinner table, but especially the littlest one.

She wasn't sure she'd ever be able to eat Sarah's mutton stew again. A sheep wasn't that different from a goat. For that matter, neither was a cow or a deer. Maybe she should embrace a vegetarian lifestyle. She did enjoy a good hamburger though.

Only ninety days old.

She wanted to ask Benjamin Mast how he could bear to sell the goats huddled in front of them. She held her tongue, though, because she remembered Sarah's words. *Try not to be emotional about it.*

Stink. How was she supposed to remain detached when Benjamin's goats were staring at her, pleading their case with their little cute eyes?

She turned her attention back to the questions she'd written down. "Tell me about the pasture they were raised in."

"Well, you've been to my place for church service, Ada. I keep the goats in the north pasture and rotate them to the east then south so they'll have plenty to eat." He smiled at one of the bigger goats that had stepped closer. The goat's ear had been tagged with the number 248. "These goats have had a *gut* life. You don't need to worry about that."

Benjamin lowered his voice. "I heard what happened with that litter of beagle puppies, and I think you did the right thing. No dog should have to spend its life in a puppy mill. I'm glad you intervened—that showed real compassion."

"*Danki.*"

"*Gem gschehne.*"

Benjamin really was a nice guy. He'd been friends with her *dat* for as long as she could remember. But those goats! To think that some had taken their first steps only three months earlier.

She cleared her throat. "Do you plan to buy more goats?"

"*Nein.* We have plenty more. Goats have two to three kids at a time, and they can give birth three times in two years. Raising goats is a *gut* source of income because they keep multiplying and they sell well."

"Have you…um…ever thought of raising goats for milk?"

Benjamin smiled broadly. "We have a dairy cow for that."

"Okay. Well, some goats are also raised for their fiber. I was reading up on it just last night—Angora and Pygora goats are *gut* for that."

"Huh. That's great to know. Well, if that's all the questions you have, I best go over to Ethan and get my paperwork sorted out."

"Oh. Okay."

"You have a *gut* day."

"You too, Benjamin."

But it didn't seem like she was headed in the right direction as far as her day was concerned. She didn't know what she'd expected, but on one level she had hoped that she was making a difference. How was she supposed to do that though? There were no puppies among the lots to rescue. All of the animals looked as if they'd been taken care of in a compassionate way.

She tried to talk to an *Englisch* rancher about his pigs, but he wasn't interested in answering her questions at all. His cell phone rang and he simply walked away as he spoke into it.

She didn't even know what questions to ask about the cattle, and certainly there was nothing to protest about the hay that was to be sold by the ton.

What was she supposed to be doing?

Why was she there?

There were no puppies to save, and she wasn't going to convince a rancher to make any drastic changes. Her mood plummeted and she began to think that she'd be better off selling popcorn, when Bishop Ezekiel waved her down.

"I heard you might have a pup to sell."

"Actually, I have seven."

"Can't say as I need that many, but I have been thinking that I'd enjoy having a dog around the place."

That was how she ended up having a late-morning cinnamon pretzel and cup of coffee with the bishop, and in the process, pouring out her heart to the dear old man.

"Each day we do the best we can, Ada. That's all the Lord expects of us."

She walked back to the auction barn realizing that she wasn't going to save animals every day. That wasn't her job. Her job was to be on the lookout for any type of neglect and then report that neglect to Gideon or Ethan.

She couldn't save every animal's life, but maybe…maybe she could save one. She rushed back into the auction barn in search of Benjamin Mast.

* * *

Ethan looked up to see Ada walking toward him, holding a lead rope that had been fastened around the neck of a small Boer goat. He tried to stifle a groan, but it must have escaped because Gideon started laughing.

"Wonder how I'm going to get that home," Gideon said.

"I wonder how she's going to pay for it." Ethan started riffling through the paperwork to find Benjamin Mast's forms.

"Hi, Gideon."

"Ada."

Ethan was tempted to walk away, but this was part of his job—dealing with difficult customers and employees. "I see you have a goat," he said by way of greeting. "I assume it's one of Benjamin Mast's."

"It is."

Ethan breathed out heavily, the sigh sounding overly dramatic even to his ears. "And you're keeping it?"

"I am."

Ethan waited, unsure what to ask next. Fortunately, Ada wasn't one to abide a silence and jumped right in.

"There wasn't any neglect, of course. Benjamin's goats all look very healthy." She paused as she stared at the goat. "This one is the smallest, and he kept staring at me with those beautiful eyes. I couldn't save them all, but I could save one."

Refusing to be pulled into Ada's odd view of the world, Ethan tried to keep his tone all-business. "Did you pay him for the goat?"

Something between frustration and anger flashed in her eyes. "I made arrangements."

She reached into her apron pocket. Setting a five-dollar bill and a one-dollar bill next to his clipboard, she said, "I believe your commission would have been six dollars per head."

Ethan nodded. She'd done her homework. An auctioneer's commission on goats was six dollars per head. He slipped the money into his pocket and changed the number of goats on Benjamin's form.

Gideon had squatted in front of the goat. "Looks like you'll be joining the Yoder family farm."

"Yoder/Fisher family farm," she reminded him. "You're in on this too—farming I mean. Not necessarily goat raising."

"Have you told your *dat*?"

"*Nein*. He'll only remind me that this little one is my responsibility, which I fully realize. Do you think I can keep him in the stall with the pups?"

"I think we can work something out. I'll just

put him in the back until we're ready to head home."

That left Ethan standing there staring at Ada. He didn't know what to say. He was completely clueless when he was around Ada Yoder, and it wasn't—as his *bruder* had suggested—because he was attracted to her. It was because they inhabited different worlds.

"Any other problems?"

"*Nein*. All the animals seem very healthy. I can't spot any concerns that a buyer might have."

Technically, that was Gideon and Ethan's job. Why had Amos insisted on Ada working with them? What was she going to do every day?

Ada must have been thinking the same thing, because she turned to go—shoulders slumped, a frown marring her pretty face. She didn't even say goodbye. It was so unlike her that Ethan felt the pull of sympathy. There'd been a time while he was living in Ohio when he hadn't known what he was supposed to do with his life. That was before his *mamm* had called them home. Before she'd asked them to rescue the family farm. Certainly before his *mamm* and *dat* had deeded the house and land to him and Aaron, then moved away.

He fully understood that he was supposed to be a *gut* steward of that farm and help provide, as best as he could, for his *bruder*'s family. But he also understood the struggle that Ada was dealing with. At least, he thought he did. He cleared his throat. "You'll figure it out."

She turned toward him, eyes widened.

"What you're supposed to do…with your life. You'll figure it out. Sometimes it just takes a while."

"Oh, I wouldn't be too sure of that. After all, I've been taking and losing jobs for six years now."

"Maybe you're going to be a rancher. You already have seven pups and one goat."

"Six pups—Bishop Ezekiel purchased one. It's how I had the six dollars to give you."

"You sold a hunting dog for six dollars?"

"*Nein.* I told him to pay what he could, and he offered fifty dollars, which seemed fair to me. I looked it up, and breeders sell them for a lot more, but then I'm not looking to make a profit. I just want to find *gut* homes for them."

"He paid you fifty dollars?"

"*Ya.* The rest is going to purchase dog food… and whatever supplies I need for a goat." She shifted from one foot to the other then looked up at him and smiled. "I'm learning that rescuing animals isn't exactly as easy as eating a piece of apple pie."

He didn't know what to say to that, so he didn't say anything. Ada offered him a little wave, which he returned even though it felt foolish to do so. Then she turned and walked away. He watched until she was out of site, until she'd traversed the long aisle in the auction barn and turned the corner.

He tried to tell himself that it didn't matter if she worked at the auction or if she decided to pursue animal rights as her career path. Ada Yoder was not his concern. He had six dollars in his pocket for the goat she'd purchased—same as if the goat had sold with the lot. It should really make no difference to him at all if Ada decided to purchase one of every animal in the auction barn.

He'd risen early that day and reviewed the financial plan for the farm. The loss of their crops had definitely hurt, but if he did well, his work at the auction barn would nearly make up for it. Bethany and Aaron's *boppli* was due the week before Christmas. Hopefully they would add on a room by then, but even if they had to wait until spring, that would be acceptable.

Apparently, it was fairly common for infants to stay in the room with their parents. Even Gideon and Becca were doing it, though they had plenty of room. They'd recently moved into a separate house on the Yoder property, one that Gideon had been working on over the last year and a half.

When Ethan asked Gideon why they'd keep the *boppli* in the room with them, Gideon had grinned and shrugged. "Because it'll make Becca happy, and that's important to me."

"Guess I don't know much about infants," Ethan admitted.

"Neither do I, but according to Sarah, it's normal for new moms to keep their *boppli* close." Gideon had laughed, probably because of the look of confusion on Ethan's face.

He was puzzled about so many things—marriage, life, infants. "So, you're telling me that's normal, regardless how big or small the house is.

"I guess. I'm not sure. This is my first experience with an expecting wife."

The main difference, to Ethan's way of thinking, was that Gideon and Becca were choosing to keep the *boppli* in their room. Aaron and Bethany wouldn't have much choice.

Still, spring would come and their financial situation would improve, and they'd add on a room. At that point, his new niece or nephew could have their own space.

Their house was crowded with only the two bedrooms, but they were able to make it work. In the back of his mind, Ethan wondered what would happen if he married. Where would their *boppli* go? But he was getting way ahead of himself. He couldn't even think of a woman he was interested in dating, let alone marrying. No one at their church gatherings had struck him as someone he should ask out. Certainly no one at work had caught his attention—except for Ada, and that wasn't the kind of attention that he was talking about.

Ada was alternately a puzzle and a pain.

He hadn't met a single woman whom he looked forward to seeing every day, whom he'd want to ask out for a buggy ride, whom he would consider bringing home for dinner.

Maybe he never would meet that person.

Maybe he was destined to be alone.

Chapter Four

Ada made a vow that she would stop adopting animals. She even wrote it in her journal and underlined it—*No More Animals!* She'd managed to find homes for five of the pups, though two of those she simply gave away. That left her with two girls whom she named Ginger and Snap. She'd always loved gingersnap cookies, and she loved the two little beagles.

They were still clumsy like the puppies they were, but they also seemed to grow bigger every day. Both had white feet, white muzzles and a white tip to their tail. Ginger had a big splash of black fur across her back and belly. Snap had one brown ear and one black. They were easy to tell apart. When Ada would walk into the horse stall every morning to set them free for the day, they would tumble around her feet until she sat and played with them. Even their old dog Gizmo seemed to enjoy them, though he often lay dozing in the sun and watching them with one eye open and the other closed.

Ada loved having both Ginger and Snap. She didn't regret for one minute having rescued them, but paying for two dogs was another matter entirely. The cost of food certainly added up. Pups ate more than she would have thought possible. Then there was the trip to the veterinarian to get their shots. Those two things combined had cost her a third of the money she'd made at the market. And, to her surprise, one goat was proving as expensive as two dogs.

Pogo was beyond adorable. He had a white streak from the top of his head to the bottom of his chin. The rest of his face and ears were brown, and then of course his body was white. He had such sweet eyes that every time she saw him, she dropped what she was doing and went over to give him a solid hug or scratch between his ears. Pogo was a very affectionate and very intelligent goat. She was sure all goat farmers said that of their goats, but in this case, she was right.

The problem was the money, or the lack of it. Why did everything have to cost so much? Feed and supplements for Pogo used up another third of her cash, which meant that she didn't have much money left at all.

The *youngies* from her church were going to a music and art festival over in Middlebury on Saturday. She didn't want to miss that. She didn't want to work all the time.

Pogo nudged her hand then bounced away.

She laughed. How could she not laugh? Pogo reminded her of when she was young and had a pogo stick. It had been purple and green, and she could bounce across the entire pasture on that thing.

Her *dat* leaned out the window of the buggy and whistled.

"Coming." She made sure the gate to the pasture was latched and then ran to catch up with her *dat*.

"Are you looking forward to the auction today?"

"Oh, *ya*. Did you know that Adam Schwartz is selling all three of his camels today?"

"Is that so?"

"It is, and you don't have to look at me that way. I do not plan on bringing home a camel."

"Good thing. I'm pretty sure it wouldn't fit in the buggy."

Ada loved her *dat*. She loved that he didn't make fun of her for her passions. He was rather strict. For instance, he hadn't helped one bit with the cost of the dogs or the goat. She supposed once you were old, being strict made sense.

When you were Ada's age, you just wished people would lighten up a little, maybe throw a quarter in the jar to help.

She'd set a donation jar on the counter of the payment stand in the auction house. She'd even spent a full hour designing a cover for it—Help the Animals—colored in purple and featuring two beagles and a goat. So far, the jar was empty.

"Are things better between you and Ethan?"

Ada made a face. Her *dat* laughed, which had been the reason she'd made the face. She loved making him laugh.

"Yes and no. *Yes*, things are better in that he's not mad at me anymore. But *no* in that he still thinks I'm foolish."

"And how do you know that?"

"The expression on his face. Ethan looks like he has a stomachache most of the time—at least, most of the time he's around me."

"Ethan is a *gut* man. He has a lot on his shoulders."

"Like what?"

"Trying to work off the debt for the farm his parents left him."

"Oh. I didn't realize he owed money on it."

"I've talked with both Ethan and Aaron," her *dat* said. "Growing up in their family was quite hard."

"Don't they love their parents?"

"I'm sure they do, but sometimes love can be heavy."

She didn't understand that at all, and it must have shown on her face because her *dat* patted her hand and murmured, "Let's pray you never have to learn that particular lesson."

"Ethan certainly looks like he's carrying around something heavy. He's all frowns and sighs. I think he feels responsible for Bethany's *boppli* too. He said something about it needing its own room. Why would a *boppli* need its own room?"

"Perhaps he's worried that Bethany and Aaron need their privacy."

"Oh." Ada suddenly realized what her *dat* was talking about. "Oh!"

"And then one infant is usually followed by another and another..."

"You don't have to remind me. I worked at the school for an entire year, remember?"

"I do."

"You're barking up the wrong power pole if you're trying to tell me about the trials of marriage. Uh-uh. Nope. Not interested."

"Some people don't see marriage as a trial, and I'm pretty sure your *schweschdern* consider having children to be a blessing."

"I guess. But can you imagine me going to the music festival this weekend dragging along a kid

or two in a stroller? How would I play Frisbee or
visit vendor booths or simply lie in the sun on a
blanket with my eyes closed? Nope. No thank
you. I need to sew my wild corn first."

Her *dat* smiled then reached over and again
patted her hand.

He understood her. Or at least he seemed to.

Ethan King, on the other hand, was a different
matter entirely. She had the strongest feeling that
he wished she didn't work at the auction at all.

Ada especially loved Wednesdays at the auction house. There were lots of people milling
about on Wednesdays. She was beginning to rec-
ognize that some were regulars and others were
there for the first time. And then there were the
animals—so many animals. All different types
and sizes and shapes. Different colors. But she'd
never really seen an animal in a pouty mood.
Even though they were being sold, they munched
contentedly at their feed or lay in a spot of sunshine.

She enjoyed that portion of her new job im-
mensely.

The ranchers seemed to be growing used to
her and her questions. Mostly, they would smile,
answer her concerns, and assure her that the
animals had been well cared for. Occasionally
someone was rude and walked away without answering her questions, but that was rare, and Ada

figured you always had to put up with a few sour lemons in your pie.

Wednesday's auction was well attended, the bidding was lively, and people seemed to be in a fine mood.

Adam Schwartz's three camels were purchased by a man who had a drive-through animal safari in Fort Wayne. Ada loved the idea of *Englischers* puttering through in their little cars, rolling down their windows, and petting a camel. She'd even like to do it in a buggy!

In addition to the camels, there was the usual assortment of cows, goats and even a few sheep being sold. She'd have liked to buy one or two of the sheep, but just thinking about how little money was in her dresser drawer at home stopped her.

The morning went well.

Ada thought she did a good job helping with the animals. She was also happy to see a younger girl from their church pushing the popcorn cart. She didn't miss that job at all.

During a break between two auctions lots, Ada walked over to the payment counter and picked up her donation jar. James shrugged in apology. The jar was still disturbingly empty. She turned back to the auction and, as she did, an *Englisch* cowboy stepped close to the auction ring.

She'd seen him talking with Ethan earlier. He had donkeys to auction because he was selling the farm and moving to Indianapolis. Ada supposed there was nowhere to put a donkey in the big city. He was a nice man, and after hearing him speak with Ethan that morning, she hadn't been able to think of a single thing to ask him. It was obvious that he cared about the donkeys as he'd named them all and was insistent that they go to good homes.

Ethan started the bidding and one after another, the half dozen donkeys were purchased. All except for one completely white foal that stood in the corner of the auction area, her lead rope tied to the rail. She seemed rather oblivious to what was going on around her, but still Ada's heart went out to the little donkey.

Was it younger than the others?

Why was it so small?

"The last donkey in this lot is not really an auction item at all," Ethan said. "As a service to Mr. Formby, we're offering this miniature albino foal for free. Matilda is in *gut* physical shape at nine months of age."

Ethan went on in that vein for a few moments, but no one offered to take the little foal. Ada was aware of that growing feeling of turmoil in her stomach. She usually had the same feeling when she was about to make a mistake, but certainly giving a donkey a home couldn't be a mistake. How could no one want it? The little thing was so cute and barely larger than a dog.

She forgot all about the music festival.

She forgot about her promise to herself not to purchase another animal.

In that moment the only thing she could think about was a little miniature donkey named Matilda. She raised her hand, shouted, "I'll take it," and hurried toward the front of the auction area.

The day had been going so well that Ethan had almost forgotten about Ada. Yes, he'd spotted her in the crowd every now and then, chatting to a rancher or smiling at a baby. One time she'd even held a woman's miniature Chihuahua while the woman purchased popcorn—as if the animal couldn't simply stand on the ground for that amount of time.

Maybe he hadn't forgotten about her, but he had stopped worrying about her…until she'd spied the donkey. He'd tried to hurry things along. He'd tried to will her attention away and toward something else. Ada's gaze locked on that animal—a blind miniature donkey.

It was exactly what Ada Yoder did not need.

Then she'd said, "I'll take it," and rushed toward the front of the bidders.

A good bit of the crowd had been about to leave since the miniature donkeys were the last lot. No one was in a hurry though. Folks liked hanging out in an auction barn on a beautiful October day, and many had stayed though they had no use for miniature donkeys. Who did? Now they watched on in amusement as Ada hurried over to where the donkey waited. She reached through the fence, let the donkey smell her hand, and smiled brightly when it licked her palm. Then she noticed the jar she was carrying, shook it as if to confirm it was empty and glanced around at the crowd.

It was like watching a train wreck that he was powerless to stop.

Ada spied a wooden crate and, faster than a rabbit pops into a hole, she had turned it over, stood on it and raised her jar in the air. "Wouldn't you good people like to have a hand in supporting this fine donkey?"

There was some laughter, but they quieted as she held the jar higher. "I've been told that I might have sparrows in my belfry…"

The laughter increased.

"I'm not really sure what a belfry is," she said in a mock whisper. "But I know that this donkey is one of *Gotte*'s creatures and deserves a *gut* home. I'm happy to take it with me, but I'm afraid I'm rather low on funds."

"The donkey is free," someone shouted from the back of the now-growing crowd.

"True enough, but I've already rescued seven beagle pups and a Boer goat, and let me tell you…free adds up to a lot of money."

Ethan fought the urge to groan as *Englischers* and Amish alike started reaching for their wallets.

He couldn't believe it.

She'd done it again.

She'd made his auction the laughingstock of the day.

Ethan told himself what Ada Yoder did was none of his business. He reined in his temper, fought to remember what he was supposed to be doing, and thanked everyone for attending the auction. Then he made his way over to the payment center. He answered questions and helped take payments. And he tried very hard not to listen to the conversation between Ada and the cowboy. The guy looked like he'd stepped out of a Western movie—his hat was a Stetson, his belt buckle large and shiny, and his boots leather. He seemed to be quite taken with Ada, but then, who wouldn't be? Anyone who didn't know her would find her charming and, of course, she was beautiful.

"I can't thank you enough for taking her."

"Well, no one else seemed to want her."

"Probably because she's blind."

"Excuse me?"

Ethan fought the urge to slap his forehead.

"Albino donkeys usually have poor eyesight. Matilda can see shadows, but not much more."

"Oh, I didn't realize."

"But you still want her, right?"

"Of course, but, um, what do I do with her?"

"Generally donkeys are purchased to be companion animals, but Matilda…well, she's not much of a companion since she's—"

"Nealry blind. Right. I get it."

The cowboy smiled at Ada, even reached up and tipped his stupid Stetson. Ethan couldn't stand there silently for another minute.

"Ada, you don't have to take that donkey. Obviously you did not understand what you were buying. In fact, it wasn't a purchase since no money exchanged hands."

She looked at him as if he were wearing his suspenders backward. "I know I don't have to take her, Ethan. But she's already bonded to me."

The blind donkey was pressing up against Ada's side as if afraid that Ethan would pull her away.

"It seems to me that Ada…" The cowboy turned and smiled, "May I call you Ada?"

"*Ya.* For sure and certain, it's my name."

Cowboy-dude smiled at Ada then turned back

to Ethan. "Seems she knows what she wants, and she wants Matilda."

"I do."

Ethan expected the two to high-five.

Instead, Ada put a hand on the top of Matilda's head and smiled up at the cowboy. "Thank you again."

Why was she thanking him?

She had done him a favor.

"No problem. And you call me at that number I gave you if you have any questions at all."

"I will." She pulled on the lead rope, gingerly turning Matilda and walking her out of the auction barn.

The cowboy sauntered off in the opposite direction, though twice he glanced back at Ada.

Ethan couldn't believe what he'd just seen. Though he had tried, he most certainly had not reined in his emotions. He'd put a lid on them, and that lid was about to blow sky high. In fact, he thought his hat might pop right off his head.

He turned to look at James, who shrugged and said, "We're done here, if you need to go."

He shook his head no, changed it to yes, and hurried after Ada. It was amazing how fast a woman and a blind donkey could walk. He caught up with her outside the auction barn as she was headed toward the main office.

"Taking your new donkey to meet your *dat*?"

She stopped, stared up at the sky for a moment and then turned on him like a winter storm bearing down on his location. Ethan at least had the good sense to back up a step.

"What is your problem, Ethan King? Why do you care if I bought a donkey?"

"I care that you're making a laughingstock out of my auction."

"People were laughing? Is that the problem? They were having fun?"

"You know what I mean."

"I do not," she said emphatically, raising the jar of donated money and shaking it at him. "They were helping, and they were happy, and you're just upset that everything worked out okay."

"Except you now have a blind donkey to care for."

"Oh, you make me so mad." She squinted her eyes. Her lips formed a straight line and she leaned in closer to him. "You're making me as mad as a yellow jacket."

"Mad as a hornet?"

"You'll find out yellow jacket or hornet if you say one more word about this donkey!"

He raised his hands in surrender then…because he was beginning to realize he'd overstepped his place…and mimed buttoning his lips.

Ada stared at him a moment, turned away,

turned back, then shook her head back and forth and stared at the ground. When she finally looked up, he was surprised to see that she was laughing.

He did not understand women. He couldn't fathom how quickly her mood had changed, but he was grateful. He was relieved. He realized that had been a close one, though he wasn't sure what exactly he'd been close to experiencing. He could actually feel sweat running down the back of his neck.

"She's so adorable." Ada stared at the donkey then scratched between its ears. The donkey closed its eyes in apparent bliss. "I think that my *dat* will be proud that I saved her. Plus, she'll fit in the buggy easily. Everything is turning up dandelions, Ethan.

"Turning up roses," he whispered as she walked away.

As he made his way back into the auction building, he wondered if he had overreacted. It was possible. Seeing Ada with that cowboy had set him off. Not that he cared who Ada dated. It was her business whether she called the phone number the man had given her.

Ethan thought that perhaps he had overreacted because he was worried about the auction.

That's what he told himself anyway.

But as he drove home, he kept seeing Ada gazing fondly at the blind donkey, and he couldn't help wondering if her attitude about life was the right attitude. She didn't worry about money or what other people thought or what might happen tomorrow.

He tried not to worry about money, but still he often did.

Of course, he didn't care what other people thought unless it affected the auction. He was simply conscientious about his job.

But tomorrow…oh, he did worry about tomorrow and the day after that and the day after that.

When had he become such a worrier?

And what was he going to do about it? Because this ball of anxiety in his gut was most certainly not a healthy thing. He reached up and rubbed his temple, which felt as if a stake had been driven through it.

The headaches had started a month ago, or maybe before that. He couldn't be sure. He only knew that it wasn't something he'd had as a *youngie*. It wasn't even something he'd experienced when he had first moved back to Shipshe. He'd been relatively happy working in the fields, even with his father's shadow hanging over every step forward they managed to make.

Now his father was in Florida.

His mother was in Florida.

And he was solely responsible for the family farm. That wasn't fair though. Aaron also helped to carry that responsibility. His *bruder* was a hard worker.

So why was he always so tense?

If he were honest with himself, why did he often feel deeply unhappy? Was it his fault? Was it because of the way he thought of things? The way he approached a day's work?

Maybe Ada was right.

Maybe it was time that he lightened up a bit.

The problem was that he had no idea how to do that.

Chapter Five

Ada's family didn't seem surprised that she'd brought home a blind donkey. Eunice even offered to create a small outdoor pen where Matilda could stand in the sun but not get into any trouble. Surprisingly, her little goat Pogo seemed quite taken with the donkey and followed it everywhere. Most of the time, her beagles Ginger and Snap could be found playing nearby. Once, when Ada went to check on them, she'd found all four animals lying asleep in a heap. They reminded her of a pile of laundry... it was hard to tell where one animal ended and another began.

She almost didn't go on the Saturday outing with the other young people from church. Her animals' stall needed to be cleaned, and she needed to buy more dog food. She was standing there, wondering how long those things would take, when Eunice and Gideon walked up.

"Thought you had an outing today," Eunice said.

"*Ya*, I did. Not sure I should go. There's, you know, work to do. I need to clean up this place, and then I need to go to town and purchase more dog food."

"I can take care of the stall," Eunice offered. "You've been doing it on your own all week."

"And I can pick up the dog food." Gideon shrugged when the girls turned to stare at him. "I have to go to the feed store anyway. What time is your group leaving?"

"Noon."

"Meeting in town?"

"*Ya*. At the Cove." The Cove was a recreation center for Plain youth, built in 2015 and funded with local donations. Ada used to go there rather often, but less in the last few months. She felt she'd outgrown the place. Still, it was a good spot to meet up.

"I can drop you off on my way to the feed store. Need to leave in thirty minutes though."

"You all are the best. I suppose I would like to go. I better break a foot, though, if I'm going to be ready on time." She headed for the house, turned back around, retraced her steps and patted each of the animals on the head, hugged

Eunice and squeezed Gideon's hand. Then she hustled toward the house.

Yes!

She had a day off. No work. No animals to worry about. No Ethan King to glare at her. She put on her dark green dress, which still looked nice even if it was a year old. It would have been a real waste of money to buy new fabric. Her paltry salary was much better spent on animals. Plus, animals were a good investment. She wouldn't outgrow animals like she would a dress.

She made it to the parking area of the rec center in plenty of time. There were already half a dozen of her friends there, and Ada found herself throwing off the burden of pet ownership like an old faded sweater.

The driver showed up on time.

Everyone was in high spirits.

And the festival was perfect. The musicians were good, the food was even better, and the weather held. No, the problem, she realized as the afternoon seemed to drag on interminably... the problem wasn't the festival. The problem was Ada.

She looked at a family with a toddler and a puppy and she wondered what Ginger and Snap were doing.

She saw an older gentleman with a service

dog, and she wondered if Matilda needed a person to keep her company.

When a young boy bounced by her on a pogo stick, she couldn't believe it. She hadn't seen one of those in years, and yet now she had a goat named Pogo.

This day seemed destined to make her miss her animals.

She finally plopped down on a blanket someone in her group had brought, lay back and threw an arm over her eyes. This is what she'd daydreamed about…hanging out with friends and resting in the sun.

It was no good though.

She simply could not relax.

She sat up, yanked her *kapp* strings to the front and began worrying them.

"What's up, Ada?" James Lapp collapsed beside her on the blanket. He was holding a paper tube covered with cotton candy in one hand and a soda in the other. "Want some?"

She reached out and pulled off some of the cotton candy—it was pink, sticky, and oh-so-good.

"I'm surprised you're here, James. You're even older than me."

"We're not that old."

"I guess."

"To tell you the truth, I'm here because I heard

Stephanie was coming, but now she's off with Noah."

He looked so miserable that Ada knew she needed to reassure him. "She doesn't like Noah in the way you're afraid she might. They're just friends."

"You're sure?"

"Yup." She pulled off another piece of the cotton candy. The sugar was improving her mood. "They grew up next door to each other. They're more like family than girlfriend-boyfriend."

"I had kind of hoped that was the case, but I was afraid to ask."

"If you don't ask, how will you know?"

"*Gut* point." He sipped from the soda then asked, "How are your animals?"

"Fine." She glanced around. "I miss them."

James started to laugh, so she reached out and slapped his arm.

"I get it," he said. "When my parents bought a new buggy horse, I stayed home with that mare every weekend."

"And now?"

He shrugged. "I still like her, but I don't see her much between work and church and stuff."

"Gosh. I don't want that to happen to me. I don't want to get too busy for Matilda."

"You've found your calling."

"I have?"

"Seems like it. Your face..." He raised a hand and waved circles around her face. It was rather like being assaulted by a butterfly. "It lights up when you're working with the animals."

"Oh. Maybe so."

"Too bad it irritates Ethan so much." James laughed again.

"I don't understand that. Why does he even care whether I'm there or not?"

James looked uncomfortable and suddenly became very interested in slurping the last drops of soda out of his cup.

"What?"

"What what?"

"What are you not telling me?"

"I don't know what you're talking about."

"James...spill it."

He sighed heavily. "I just think he likes you."

"What?" The word came out three times louder than she'd intended. She thrust the cotton candy back at him, stood and brushed the wrinkles from her dress. "I think you've been out in the sun too long."

"I've been sitting here in the shade with you."

"Well, your mind is tipsy-turvy if you think that Ethan King likes me." She strode off, spied Stephanie and Noah walking back toward their blanket of stuff, turned and stomped back to

James. Dropping onto the blanket, she leaned in and whispered, "Now's your chance."

"Chance for what?"

"To ask Stephanie to go and get a soda or something."

"I just finished a soda."

"James..." She drew the word out then shook her finger back and forth. "Either you ask her, or I'll go tell her how you feel."

"Why would you do that?"

"Because you need a little, you know...push." And with that she reached forward and pushed him over.

He looked embarrassed and unsure of himself, but he stood and said, "Fine. I'll ask her. Just for you."

"Danki."

He flashed her a smile, and then he was gone.

Ada hopped up and hurried off in the opposite direction. She didn't want to watch. She also didn't want Noah to get any ideas about asking her for a soda. The friends she hung out with were all nice, but she thought of them as family. They were like one big litter of puppies—playful and cozy and not scary at all.

There was nothing romantic about it. She did not think of the guys *that* way. She wasn't sure she'd ever thought of any man *that* way.

She wandered through the crowd, and her

thoughts drifted back to Pogo and Matilda, Ginger and Snap. The money she'd raised had helped, but those critters would eat through it in no time. She needed another way to support them. She needed another job to support them.

Suddenly she found herself standing in front of a table with cute photos of puppies and dogs. The banner on the front of the table read "SPCA, Society for the Prevention of Cruelty to Animals." She'd probably seen them around before, but she'd never stopped to read one of their pamphlets. There was also a donation jar on the table that was stuffed with money. How did they raise money? How did they convince people to contribute, not just once, but on a regular basis?

Maybe those answers were in the colorful pamphlets.

"Go ahead and take one. They're free."

"*Ya?* You're sure?"

"I'm sure," said the gray-haired woman who was sitting behind the table. She leaned forward and lowered her voice as if to share a big secret. "It's literally why we're here."

"*Danki.*" Ada remembered to smile as she picked up a pamphlet then walked away.

A charitable organization.

That just might be what she needed.

After all, she couldn't depend on what random strangers were willing to stick in a mason jar. She needed steady donations—maybe even sponsorships from local businesses.

She'd have to call it something different than SPCA though.

Something about animals and auctions and caring for them. Not too long either. She ran her fingers over the glossy pamphlet. She couldn't afford to make anything as fancy as the SPCA had, but she could make up a single sheet that could go into windows. Bethany was good at making stuff. She'd probably love to help.

Ada's mood lifted. She glanced up and saw a kite, followed the string down to the young girl who was learning how to fly it. Her *dat* stood behind her, encouraging her, cheering her on.

That was what Ada's family did for her.

Unlike Ethan King, who only seemed to criticize. He definitely did not like her in the way that James had suggested. What had ever given him that idea? She did want to have that sort of relationship with someone. She wanted a family like Becca and Bethany had. She wanted to care for a family like Sarah did. She wanted to constantly be thinking of ways to help her family like Eunice did.

The problem was that she didn't feel that way about anyone she knew. You were supposed to get all flushed and dizzy and at a loss for words. She only felt flushed when she had a fever or

Ethan made her angry. The same was true for the only times she'd ever felt slightly dizzy. As for being at a loss for words, that hadn't happened to her yet except when she tried to come up with a snappy retort for Ethan.

Ethan! Why did every path her mind traipsed lead back to him? She worried she might be acquiring attention deficit disarray.

With great determination, she pushed all thoughts of Ethan from her mind and turned her attention back to her animals, what she could do to support them, and how her family might help.

They wanted to see her be successful.

She didn't doubt for a minute that they would help.

A charitable organization might be just the ticket.

She should have thought of that before.

Ethan made a valiant attempt to lighten up over the next few days. He laughed at his *bruder*'s jokes, tried not to worry about money, and he even managed to tolerate Ada's misquotes when they went to the Yoder home for Sunday luncheon.

He avoided her, to be sure, but he smiled with everyone else when she brought out her animals and showed the family how she'd taught them to follow her. "See? I've finally got my ducks in a circle."

They were in a sort of circle, until the blind donkey stopped, the goat bleated then tried to nab the tablecloth on the picnic table, and the dogs proceeded to attack Amos's shoes. Amos laughed with everyone else. Ethan laughed then pressed a finger to his throbbing temple. Though it was a cool October day, the sun seemed inexplicably bright. He should have brought sunglasses. He never wore sunglasses, but maybe he should start.

His mood turned even darker as the afternoon wore on.

He saw Bethany and Becca standing together, both looking as if they could give birth any day. What if he and Aaron weren't ready? What if next year's crops succumbed to another natural disaster? What if he couldn't handle working at the farm and working at the auction?

Ethan felt tired and out of sorts. He didn't want to be a cranky young man who turned into a cranky old man. He sure didn't want other people to think of him that way. He tried to smile at all the appropriate places and thought he was doing a pretty good job of keeping his dark mood to himself, until Gideon asked, "Say, are you feeling okay? You look a little...pale."

He looked pale?

He was a farmer. He had a farmer's tan. Didn't he?

"Fine... I'm fine. Just didn't sleep well is all."

Gideon nodded, slapped him on the back and then went off in search of an extra piece of pie.

Ethan was more than relieved when Bethany admitted she could use a nap and they all decided to go home early. He had given a better attitude his best shot, but everything felt like such an effort. That afternoon and evening he hung out in the barn—though technically they didn't work on Sunday. Still, the barn felt like where he should be. There wasn't really anything to do there, but just being around the horses helped a little.

His headaches were becoming more pronounced, and he started to wonder if there was something wrong with him—like, physically wrong with him. That only gave him one more thing to be uptight about, which made the headaches worse. He was caught in a vicious loop.

It didn't help that they'd received a letter from the bank asking that they come in and speak to a loan officer. Aaron needed to be at the market the next day. Mondays were always busy with new campers coming in and old ones checking out. Ethan said he'd take care of going to the bank. He'd do it before work—first thing. Get it over with, like the terrible-tasting cough syrup he'd occasionally endured as a child.

He told himself as he dressed for work Monday morning to be more optimistic. He needed to have a better attitude going into a new week.

Aaron and Bethany took the newer buggy with the newer horse into the market. Bethany was wanting to spend one last week at work, though no one was sure that was a *gut* idea. Often they would all ride in together, but Aaron pulled Ethan aside and said, "I think we should take separate buggies, just in case Bethany wants to come home at lunch."

"I'm not sick," she called out. The woman possessed unnaturally good hearing. "I'm only pregnant."

Ethan hitched Misty to the older buggy and took it to the bank. The loan officer was a Mrs. Garcia—older and short, her long black hair pulled back with a hairband. He thought at first that she seemed quite severe. She studied his records on her computer, a somber and focused look on her face. Finally, she sat back, regarded him and smiled.

"We're pleased to see that you've been able to keep up with the payments owed."

"*Ya*. It's very important to us—to me and my *bruder*—to take care of that."

"And I see that you two now own the farm."

"That's right. My parents, they moved to Florida and sold the farm to us."

When she steepled her fingers together and waited, he pushed on.

"For a sum of one dollar. *Mamm* said that

made it official. Aaron and I are working hard to pay off the loan and make improvements on the place."

"I'm sure the weather this year has not been helpful in that regard. In fact, that's why we sent out the letters to all of our agricultural clients with outstanding loans. We'd rather get in front of a problem than get bowled over by it later."

"What kind of problem?"

"Let me ask you a question. Do you anticipate any trouble in making future payments?"

"*Nein*. I mean no, we don't."

She waved toward the window, where clouds skidded across the sky and a strong northerly wind pushed the branches of the trees. "And yet you haven't been able to bring in a crop this year. Many farmers weren't able to. Those who don't have crop insurance, and I'm guessing you don't—"

Ethan shook his head. As a member of the Amish church, they didn't believe in insurance of any type. They helped one another with their tithes and offerings. It was what they'd always done.

"Without crop insurance...well, we can hope next year will be better, but there's no guarantee."

"True." Ethan sat straighter, realizing suddenly where she was going with this line of discussion. "Aaron and I both work at the market."

"Oh." She leaned forward and peered at her computer, clicked the mouse a few times then cocked her head. "I see here that Aaron King has been working for the market for some time, but I didn't realize you were."

"When the fields were flooded, it was too late to replant. I'm glad that I didn't, since the period of rain was followed by months of drought."

"A very rare occurrence in northern Indiana."

"Right. So we knew that this year's crops were not viable, and I took a job at the market."

"And next year?"

"What do you mean?"

"I assume you can't continue to work at the market and plant new crops."

The sudden pain in Ethan's right temple caused him to squeeze his eyes shut then open them quickly. He attempted to smile. "I can do both if it's necessary."

Mrs. Garcia nodded her head and then typed something on her keyboard. She stood and held out her hand for him to shake. "It's nice to see young men with such a strong work ethic. I could use more clients like you."

He shook her hand, thanked her, then hurried back outside. Misty was right where he'd left her, though now she was dozing unfazed by the cold northern wind. Ethan took a moment to stand with the horse, rest his hand on the side of her neck and offer her a peppermint from his pocket.

He was a farmer.

Of course he would find a way to plant the spring crops.

Could he do both jobs though? That was the question, and the only answer he knew, the only answer he considered, was the one he'd offered to Mrs. Garcia.

I can do both if it's necessary.

Chapter Six

Ada didn't work at the market on Mondays. Instead, she stayed home and helped with chores. On the Monday after the park outing, she waited until her *dat* was off to the market and her *schweschdern* were in the kitchen. Once she was sure she had their attention—gained by whistling and waving her arms until everyone turned to stare at her—she presented her plan to create a charitable organization for auction animals.

Sarah said, "Hmm" and tapped a finger against her lips.

Becca glanced at Eunice then stared down at her protruding stomach.

Eunice rubbed her forehead with her fingertips.

"You're acting like I just gave you all a cold. Don't you think it's a *gut* idea?"

"Well, I guess…it could be." Sarah jumped

up, fetched the coffeepot and refilled their mugs. "Tell us again what you hope to accomplish."

So Ada went back over her entire thought process. How much free animals cost. How there always seemed to be some animal that she needed to adopt. How she'd stumbled upon the SPCA booth and had the brilliant idea to copy what they were doing. How she felt she needed to do this thing. "Not just because of cruel prospective owners...like with the dogs. Sometimes it's just someone who can no longer take care of an animal, like Matilda."

"Speaking of which..." Now Becca's eyes literally twinkled. "Have you called him yet?"

"Called who?"

"The man who gave you Matilda."

"Why would I call him?"

Now her three *schweschdern* looked at each other and smiled. It made Ada want to stomp her foot. She hated not being in on a joke. Since it felt strange to stomp your foot while you were sitting—she had tried it before and no one had even noticed—Ada sat back and crossed her arms tightly.

"Uh-oh. She's got that expression on her face," Eunice said.

"I don't see what's so funny is all."

"Ada." Sarah gave her that motherly look that always made her feel both better and worse at the same time. How was that possible? "When a man gives you his phone number, it's because he's interested."

"Interested?"

"In you…" Eunice offered.

"In dating you," Becca clarified.

"That's crazy, and you're wrong. Joe Formby—that's the name on the card—gave me his number in case I had questions about Matilda."

"*Ya*, that's what he said." Becca smiled brightly. "But sometimes a man will say that so you'll call and then that's when he asks you out on a date."

She thought they were pulling her apron strings, but all three were now staring at her and waiting. "Seriously?"

"*Ya*. Happened to me once when I was lending a hand in the diner at the market." Eunice sipped her coffee. "I was clearing off tables and a man handed me his card. I guess they realize we don't have phones to pop their number into. He gave me the card and said something like 'Call me if you ever need a tiny house.' He was a tiny house builder."

"Did you want a tiny house?"

"No, of course not, but he gave me the card all the same."

"So they walk around with these cards…just to give to women?" Ada couldn't believe this. "How strange."

Becca shook her head. "*Englischers* use them for business as well as picking up girls."

That sent them all into a fit of laughter, even Ada.

She finally wiped her eyes and said, "That's the problem though. They're *Englisch*."

And that caused Becca to rub her tummy and Sarah and Eunice and Ada to sigh. Marrying an *Englischer* would be...problematic. As Ada very well knew, since none of them ever had. Of course, dating and marrying were two different things.

"I'm not interested in Joe Formby romantically speaking."

"Didn't you say he was good-looking?" Eunice asked.

"*Ya*. He was. He is. He looked like he could star in a movie about cowboys, but I don't know..." She shrugged then admitted, "He didn't do it for me."

"Didn't do it?" Sarah smiled and waited for a more detailed explanation.

"Didn't...you know...give me moths in my stomach."

"Butterflies?"

She waved away the correction. "Let's focus, okay?"

"Wait." Eunice held up a finger. "One more question. Does anyone do it for you?"

The only time she'd ever felt that way, unsettled and confused and hopeful all at once, was when she was around Ethan…and that was probably due to his foul mood. Who wouldn't be unsettled and confused when someone was glowering at you? As for being hopeful, hope sprang daily.

"Not really. Now, about my organization…"

After she explained, again, that she'd like to raise money for needy auction animals, Eunice began jotting down notes, Sarah clarified what she hoped to accomplish, and Becca started doodling designs. It took less than an hour to glue it all down and, after lunch, Becca and Ada started working on the single-page flyers.

They made a dozen before she had to stop to go care for her animals. She liked the way that sounded—*her animals*. At dinner that night, the topic of her new organization came up again.

Sarah was the one to broach the subject, and she waited until their father was full, relaxed, and in a *gut* mood. "Explain it to *Dat*, Ada. It's actually pretty impressive."

"Okay." She glanced around at her family. They'd all finished eating—pork cutlets, mashed potatoes, steamed carrots and salad. She felt full as a flea. "I'm calling it Amish for the Humane Treatment of Auction Animals."

"Interesting name." He nodded as he sipped from his glass of water. "A bit long…"

"True, but we…" She beamed at her *schweschdern*. "We all decided better that it be long and accurate than short and catchy and misleading."

"You know, Amos, we might be able to add it to our website." Gideon was running his fingers through his beard, something he always did when he was thinking hard about a thing. "We'd need more of Ada's goals and intentions. We might even be able to add a little donate button."

"Oh! Like a fundaising page." When everyone only stared at her, Ada explained. "Not that I have a phone, but I've scrolled around on my friends' before. Sometimes on FaceNovel…"

"Facebook?" Eunice asked.

"Whatever. Sometimes they have fundraisers or charity things. It's not all gossip and cute pictures. These fundraiser posts have a button, and if you push on it then you're taken to a fundraising page. You just click and donate."

Amos was nodding, which was a *gut* thing, but he was also sitting forward with his arms crossed on the table, which could sometimes be a bad thing. "We'll need to have someone at work check into this first. See if you need to file for a 501c3."

"A what?" the girls all said at once, causing everyone to smile.

"It's a government designation that lists you as a nonprofit, so you won't be taxed on the donations. I'll call my accountant tomorrow and ask. For now, I think it would be okay to put the flyers out and schedule your first meeting. We'll have some answers by the time you actually meet."

Ada jumped up, hugged her *dat*'s neck then said, "I need to go and check on the animals." As she was snagging her sweater from the mudroom, she froze because she heard her name.

"I've never seen her this interested in anything," Sarah said.

"It's lasted longer than her interest in scuba diving or raising butterflies." That sounded like Eunice. Ada was pretty sure it was Eunice, whom she'd never been able to convince that butterflies might need raising.

"She's happy." Ah, that was Becca. If she had Becca on her side… "She's happy because she's doing something important. Those dogs would have gone to the puppy mill if she hadn't interceded. As for the goat and the donkey…well, I guess every farm can use one."

"Even if one's blind?" In spite of the question, Gideon's voice was kind, not judgmental.

"Even if it's blind."

She stepped outside feeling better even though she'd eavesdropped. She understood that eavesdropping was technically a bad thing to do, but sometimes it helped to know how your family really felt about a thing.

She thought of Ethan, wondered how he would react, and decided it probably wouldn't be good. Still, the organization she was planning had nothing to do with him. Maybe he'd have no opinion at all—that would be a nice change from the usual.

The important thing was that her family was behind her, and that was really all she needed to know. Though she was self-aware enough to realize how nice it would be if once, just once, Ethan said he was proud of her.

Ethan arrived at work still convinced that he needed to stop worrying so much. He hadn't slept well. He had a crick in his neck and he had the shadow of one of those headaches. Could he have a brain tumor? That was the last thing his family needed to deal with.

He would try being more relaxed, less tense, pleasant even.

Unfortunately, events conspired to keep any of those things from happening. How could he lighten up? Ada Yoder was actively trying to make him crazy.

He stared at the homemade flyer in his hand.

James waited, trying not to laugh. "She's tenacious. You have to give her that."

"This can't be happening."

"It's not that bad."

"It's not good."

Amish for the Humane Treatment of Auction
Animals
All are welcome to join
First Meeting: Saturday, noon, JoJo's Pretzels
Contact Ada Yoder for more information

Someone had doodled animals across the bottom and the top of the sheet. The doodling was actually pretty good. He suspected one of her *schweschdern* had done that. The Yoder girls were a talented bunch.

"Is it too much to hope this is the only one?"

"It's not."

"Not too much to hope?"

"Not the only one. She put three or four around the market and more in the downtown windows. She was here early—even beat you."

Of course, she'd arrived at the market early. Ada had been sure to get there before him because she'd known that he wouldn't have let her tape the flyer to the payment counter.

He ran into her ten minutes later, between Lot 14 and Lot 15, holding her clipboard and smiling.

"*Gudemariye*, Ethan."

He glowered at her. Ada's smile diminished considerably.

"Did you see my flyers?"

"I did."

"*Dat* said it was okay for me to post them, so I..." Her explanation drifted away as she glanced around then finally met his gaze. "You look as if you've been sucking on limes. I suppose that means you don't like them."

"The flyers are fine, Ada...if your goal is to make a laughingstock of this auction."

Instead of arguing with him, which he'd kind of hoped for—at least with an argument he stood a chance of winning, albeit with Ada a very small chance—she simply raised her chin higher, smiled tightly, pivoted on her cute little feet and headed off in the opposite direction.

At least the morning passed without her interfering with any of the auction lots. She moved easily among the ranchers now, calling them by name, squatting to pet the animals, checking things off on her clipboard.

What could she possibly be checking off?

Ethan's mood grew worse all morning and he hit rock bottom by lunch. He decided a walk would do him good and headed for the back parking area. His plan was to check on Misty, to see if there was anything she needed, and maybe sit on a bench and watch the leaves fall off the trees. But none of that worked. Oh, Misty was glad to see him, but sitting on the bench made him restless. Hearing the sound of horseshoes clanging over in the RV park irritated him. How could someone be enjoying this fine fall day when he was so miserable?

But he was always miserable.

He didn't know how he'd become this way.

He occasionally thought he might be afflicted with his *dat*'s bipolar disease, but he'd yet to have a high-energetic optimistic mood, so he didn't think that was his problem. It was just the pressure. He needed to talk to somebody. He stood and meandered back to the auction barn by way of the parking area.

Who could he speak with about his worries? About Ada?

His *bruder*? *Nein*. He didn't want to add to Aaron's troubles.

His boss? Amos wasn't exactly objective in regard to Ada.

The bishop? Maybe.

He was ruminating over that—considering names and discarding them like cards from a deck, when he nearly bumped into Sarah Yoder. Sarah was four years his senior. He'd known her in school, but not well—after all, when she'd been an eighth grader, he'd been in fourth. They'd had little in common.

"Hi, Ethan." Sarah stopped in her tracks. "What's wrong?"

"Wrong?"

"*Ya.* You don't look so good."

"People keep telling me that. It's going to hurt my feelings sooner or later."

She smiled at him. A genuine, warm smile like his own *mamm* might have given him, or a big *schweschder* if he'd had one.

"I stopped in to drop off some paperwork my *dat* left at the house. Now I'm out, on this beautiful day, and I'm not ready to go home." She ducked her head. "Walk with me?"

He couldn't think of a reason to say no, so he mumbled, "*Ya.* Sure."

They walked, and maybe that was why it was easy to talk to her. It was easier than if they'd been sitting down with all the attention on what he did or didn't say. Instead, as they moved along, beside the creek and toward the back of the RV park, he found himself pouring out his troubles to her. When he finally ran out of steam, she tucked her arm in his.

If any other girl had done that, he would have stepped away.

If Ada had done it, he would have jumped like he'd been stung by a bee.

But this was Sarah, and she was treating him like a younger sibling, like a friend. He realized in that moment that he needed a friend. Why hadn't that occurred to him before?

"Sounds as if you're under a lot of pressure."

"I suppose."

"Sometimes it helps just to get it off your chest."

"It would help more if you had some surefire answers."

She laughed, not at him but with him, which caused him to laugh too.

"I've always wanted a younger *bruder*. All those girls in our house, it's enough to make you wish for boys. We could have used a few frogs in the laundry or baseballs through the window. Instead we had five girls, counting myself. We're not a particularly dramatic bunch, but it was hard at first, after my *mamm* died. I remember feeling responsible for everyone."

"Probably because you were. Even if you weren't, you would have felt that way. My *mamm* would sometimes tell me that it wasn't my job to worry, but it was. If I didn't, who would?"

"Did worrying help at all?"

He shrugged. "Maybe not."

They'd reached a small playground that Aaron had put in at the back of the RV park. It was vacant at the moment. Sarah walked over to one of the swings and plopped onto the seat. Feeling ridiculous, Ethan sat in the swing beside hers.

"You and Aaron are doing a *gut* job. From what you just told me, the bank's loan officer said as much."

"*Ya*, but what if I can't handle both jobs? What if the crops fail again next year and I have to continue…year after year…planting crops that don't grow and working at the auction?"

"That would be a terrible future indeed." She set the swing to moving forward and back, forward and back. "Ezekiel told me once that I didn't have to believe everything I thought."

"Ezekiel said that?"

"He did."

"What does it mean?"

"I suppose it means different things to different people. To me it means that just because I think a thing, or worry over a thing, doesn't mean that I actually believe it."

"Huh."

"You might worry about the crops failing year after year, but that doesn't mean you believe they will fail year after year."

Now he nodded in agreement. Of course, he knew that crops wouldn't fail every year. If they did, who would dare to be a farmer? Indiana had suffered through very few years of low rainfall. Usually their weather was dependable. Perhaps he should think of that instead of focusing on worst-case scenarios.

"As for Bethany and Aaron, I think they will be fine."

"Then why do I worry over them so?"

"Maybe because it's out of your control."

He hadn't thought that he needed to be in control, but he supposed he sort of did. "My entire life, living with my *dat* and his condition, every day was out of control. Since we've been back... Since Aaron and I have taken over the farm, we make the decisions, and it's been nice."

"We love Aaron," Sarah admitted. "It's plain how much he cares for Beth, and we absolutely adore both of them...and we care for you. We're your family, too, Ethan."

He didn't answer that because he didn't know how, and suddenly he had trouble swallowing, which was probably due to all the leaves and the wind and allergies and such.

They stood and made their way back to the parking area. The least he could do was walk her to her buggy, since she'd spent a good half hour listening to him whine.

"What do I do about Ada?"

"What do you want to do about her?"

"I just... I want things to run smoothly here. I don't want our auction to be the laughingstock of northern Indiana."

"Do you really think my *dat* would allow that?"

"No," he answered immediately. "I don't."

Sarah smiled as if he'd answered a quiz question correctly. *Right answer, young man!* He could practically hear her encouraging her younger siblings. She'd had years and years of experience.

"But how do I get her focus off this animal thing? I mean, if Ada and I weren't running up against each other every day, things might be easier."

"It is interesting that *Gotte* has put you two together at this time in this place."

Ethan wasn't sure it was *Gotte*'s doing. Was that a thought or a belief? What had Sarah said? *Just because I think a thing, or worry over a thing, doesn't mean that I actually believe it.* Was this like that?

"Ada has a lot of energy and usually, not this time, but usually a short attention span."

"So I should just wait?"

"I didn't say that. You know we're all happy that she's finally interested in something, and if you could see her care for those animals…" She snapped her fingers. "I have an idea."

"Will I like it?"

They'd reached her buggy and the Yoder's oldest mare, Oreo.

Sarah stood there, scratching the horse's neck

but watching Ethan. "Maybe Ada needs to spend some time on area farms."

"She lives on a farm."

"True, but maybe she needs to see the other end of this thing. After all, we don't raise animals on our farm, though we may start at some point. What I'm saying is that she has no experience with that side of things."

"Huh."

"Don't you go out on farm visits?"

"*Ya.* That's part of my job. After someone contacts the auction house, we will often go out to visit, assess, and give an estimate on what we think they can expect to receive for whatever they want to sell."

"Take Ada with you." She gave Oreo a final scratch and unwound her reins from the hitching post.

"Take her with me?"

"Sure. Take her out to see the farmers, to see how hard they work raising the animals. It might…well, it might broaden her perspective a bit."

"I'm not sure that will work."

"And yet what you've tried so far certainly hasn't."

"*Gut* point."

He held the door as she climbed up into the buggy. Before he closed it, he said, *"Danki."*

"*Gem gschehne,*" she replied with a smile.

Then he shut the door, she called out to Oreo and she was gone.

Leaving Aaron standing there, wondering how he was going to invite Ada to accompany him on a farm visit and whether or not he had the courage to even give such a thing a try.

Chapter Seven

Ada thought that Ethan's offer might be a trick or a joke, but he seemed sincere.

"Sure you're not pulling my *kapp* strings?"

"*Nein*. I'd like you to go with me." He sputtered to a stop, glanced around, then added brightly, "And you might enjoy seeing the farm—you know, where the animals come from, and that sort of thing."

Ada crossed her arms and studied him. "Are you trying to talk me out of my new organization?"

He held up his hands—palms out. "Not at all."

"Hmm. Well, I don't want to sound like an eager sunfish..."

"Eager beaver?"

"But I would like to go see some of the farms." She supposed she'd been to most of them for church services, but she'd been too busy with her friends to pay any attention to the animal pens. "Okay, it's a deal. When do we leave?"

"Meet me here tomorrow morning, first thing."

"I don't usually work on Thursdays."

"True enough. I mean, if you don't want to go…"

He seemed to be getting cold fingers. Maybe he was regretting asking her. She needed to hop on this before the offer evaporated like the morning clouds. "Great. I'll meet you here…normal time."

"Excellent."

"Wunderbaar."

James Lapp walked by, gave them both a quizzical look, then began whistling and gazing up at the sky. All of which was suspicious, but Ada didn't have time to figure it out. She hurried off toward the buggy parking area. She certainly didn't want to keep her *dat* waiting.

When she told her *dat* about Ethan's offer, he didn't seem a bit surprised.

When she mentioned it at dinner, Sarah said, "I'm so glad he invited you." The way she smiled, though, you would have thought Ethan's suggestion had been her idea or something.

Ada decided to put other people out of her mind. Except that was more difficult to do than it had been when she was younger. Becca's stomach was getting so large that she feared for her.

"How do you stand it?" she asked as they sat on the front porch later that evening—Ada on the porch steps, Becca in a rocker because she couldn't possibly sit on the floor any longer.

"I just tell myself it's going to be a *boppli* soon."

"Hmm."

"Aren't you excited about having a niece or nephew?"

"I am. Sure. Yup."

"It won't be like the children you taught at school or the ones you babysat."

She hadn't wanted to bring that fear up with either Becca or Bethany. She hadn't wanted to worry them. Now she said, as casually as possible, "Those children I attempted to teach and babysit were all quite a handful."

Instead of being offended or worried, Becca simply smiled and pressed a hand to her stomach. "This baby will be different because this baby will be family."

"I'm relieved to hear you say that. Even if he or she is spoiled, I suppose we'll have to bite the bagel and love the little tyke all the same."

"Are we talking about Becca's *boppli* being spoiled?" Sarah pushed through the screen door and sat in the rocker next to Becca. "Because I can't imagine such a thing. First *boppli* we'll have had in this home since Ada."

Becca put a hand on her stomach and stared up at the ceiling of the porch. "Let's see. If I'm doing my math right, first *boppli* in nineteen years."

"Our *schweschder* probably is worried about being replaced." Sarah lowered her voice in a mock whisper. "Considering she is the youngest and all."

"I am not worried about being replaced." Ada tossed her *kapp* strings over her shoulders. She'd always been the youngest and the one everyone doted on. It got old after a while. Of course, it had its advantages too. "Besides, Bethany's *boppli* is due before yours, so it will technically be the youngest."

"Imagine that," Eunice said, joining them. "Imagine this family with two *bopplin* in the space of a few weeks."

That seemed to stun them all into silence.

Ada had trouble sleeping that night. She tossed and turned, thinking of Becca and Bethany, thinking of her trip to the farms the next day, thinking of her new organization, and finally… she was mature enough to admit it…thinking of Ethan.

She flopped on to her back and stared at the ceiling.

It was ridiculous to let any of those things keep her awake. Becca, Bethany, and both of their *bopplin* would be fine—she was sure of it. What was there to worry about? Women went into childbirth, squealing *bopplin* were born, and life went on. She tried to imagine what a niece or nephew would look like, but failed. She tried to imagine what childbirth would be like, squeezed her eyes shut and pushed the image away. She'd think of something else instead.

She'd taken the first step in establishing her new organization. There was no way to know if anyone would show up for the meeting or not. She'd have to *Let Go and Let Gotte.* Or was it *Let Jump and Let Jesus*? Honestly, she simply wasn't good about remembering sayings. Maybe the exact words didn't matter as much as the intent—which was plainly to stop worrying!

She flopped to the other side. What farms would she visit with Ethan tomorrow? Why had he really asked her to tag along? Why was he so different from how he used to be when he'd stayed with them, when his and Aaron's house had nearly burned down? He'd been the perky one then, and Aaron had been all somber and distant. It was as if they'd switched positions.

Back in those days, Aaron was still fighting the idea of being *in lieb* with Bethany. If she remembered right, Bethany had shared that he'd also been worried about having his *dat*'s bipolar disease.

Did Ethan worry about that?

She thought that was possible. Not enough sleep could make a person grumpy, and Ethan King was definitely grumpy. Perhaps he stayed awake most nights, like she was awake now. Maybe he flipped and flopped as he checked his own bad temperament against what he'd experienced with his *dat*.

That could be it. Like Aaron, he could be a perpetual worrier—about being like his *dat*, not about being *in lieb*. She couldn't think of a single girl whom Ethan liked to be around. She'd never seen him on a date before. She'd never seen him do anything but work, go to church and hang out with family.

Tomorrow wasn't a date, but still… She doubted that he knew the first thing about taking a girl for a ride to a farm. He'd probably show up in a dirty buggy with trash spilled all over the floorboards and mud splattered all over the outside. He wouldn't think about cleaning it up since this wasn't a date. This was business.

She sighed, yawned and flipped over to the other side.

What kind of woman would Ethan date? He was a fine-enough-looking fellow—nearly six feet, thin, and quite muscular since he worked in the fields or with the animals every day. When he rolled up his shirtsleeves, his arms looked like ropes. And she'd seen him pick up giant bags of feed by himself.

His brown hair was cut like all other Amish men, rather like someone had put a bowl on his head and then trimmed around it. On some men, that looked rather silly, but on Ethan, it looked just right.

There wasn't a thing wrong with how Ethan King looked. The problem was his terrible attitude.

Well, tomorrow was another time.

Perhaps he'd show up at work with a brand-new perspective, with a sunny smile, with a freshly baked donut that he'd just happened to pick up for her. That picture in her mind made her laugh, then smile, then finally drift into a peaceful sleep.

Ethan didn't show up at the market with a better attitude, though that had been his goal when he'd first rolled out of bed. Then he'd realized how dirty his buggy was and had spent twenty minutes hosing it off. The inside was nearly as bad as the outside, which meant he spent another ten minutes gathering up trash and wiping off the seats. As for Misty, there wasn't a thing he could do about her, though he thought she still looked like a fine mare. That was love talking though. To anyone else, she probably looked old and spent.

It wasn't as if he was going on a date.

He wasn't sure what he was nervous about.

Aaron and Bethany were giving each other knowing smiles, and he did not want to hang around to hear what they were saying when he left the room. The day was stressful enough. He suspected they were misreading his intentions, which was fine. He didn't care what people thought so long as his and Sarah's plan worked.

When he arrived at the market, Ada was already there waiting for him. "Did you bring a donut?" she asked brightly.

"Why would I bring a donut?"

"Oh, I don't know. Just thought you might."

"*Nein*. Didn't you eat at home?"

"I did." She turned away quickly and studied the horse.

"I need to go to the auction barn and see if we've had any more calls on the answering machine."

"Oh. Does that happen very often? Last-minute additions?"

He wished she'd worn some older clothes. It was hard to concentrate when she was wearing a pumpkin-colored dress and starched white *kapp*. She looked as if she was going to a festival rather than to a farm.

Too late, he realized she was waiting on him to respond to something she'd said.

"What?"

"Do you have very many last-minute additions?"

"It happens on occasion." They walked to the auction office together. He checked the machine's messages. There were two—one confirmed the time he would be visiting and another asked if he could come by between eleven and lunch. He had to listen to the message twice because he'd become distracted by some scent Ada was wearing.

He didn't think it was perfume—surely, it wasn't. He didn't know any Amish woman who spent money on perfume. Of course, he didn't know many Amish women that well. He pushed the entire line of thought out of his mind and made sure he'd written down all the pertinent information from the messages.

He didn't mind adding one more farm to their list of three. He thought four was a perfect number. Four farms should help Ada understand what it was like to raise animals. He hadn't even thought about the Yoders not having animals on their place. He'd lived there for a few weeks after their house had burned. He should have thought of it. He should understand Ada better than he did, but there you had it. He didn't.

It made sense that she was surprised when she saw the animals at the auction. It even made sense that she was sympathetic. All of that would change today. When she witnessed how much work and care the farmers put into raising the animals, her whole attitude would improve and maybe she would cancel the meeting for her new organization.

It was possible.

The first farm they visited was owned by Clarence Bontrager. He had a mare and a buggy that he wanted to sell. Ethan explained to Ada that the old guy's sight had worsened and he wasn't able to drive anymore.

"That's terrible."

"Happens with old folks sometimes."

"How old is he?"

"I have no idea." Ethan tried not to stare at the way she pulled on her bottom lip when she was thinking over something.

"How will he get around without a buggy or a mare?"

"He's moving soon—to Florida. Until then, neighbors stop by and give him a ride."

"Oh." She cornered herself in the buggy and stared at him, cocking her head. "How are we going to help him?"

"I'll see what condition his mare is in and take a look at the buggy. Then I'll tell him what I think those two items will bring at the auction. I'll also explain what our fee is."

"Okay. But he can't see. How will he get them there?"

"If he agrees to sell them, I'll bring James Lapp out on Monday. He can drive the buggy back…"

"Ah."

"Any other questions?" He thought she looked as if she might start taking notes at any minute, but instead she turned and stared out the window.

"It's hard. Don't you think?" After another minute passed, she turned and looked at him. "Getting too old to drive? I can't imagine such a thing. And not being able to see?"

She gestured out the window at the colored leaves on the ground and the hay in the fields and the sunshine splashing across the road. Then she fell silent.

Ethan had brought Ada on this trip because he'd wanted her to understand the farmers' perspective. Maybe that would happen. He hoped so. But he was also beginning to understand a few things about Ada Yoder. She felt things very strongly—felt sympathy for man and beast very strongly. That wasn't a bad thing. They could probably use more people like her in the world.

Mr. Bontrager turned out to be quite the character. Though he couldn't see well…which was evident by the way he craned his neck forward and peered at them…he hadn't let it slow him down one bit.

"To tell you the truth, I continued driving long past when I should have. But Sweet Girl, that's what I call my mare because she has always been the sweetest horse you'll ever have the pleasure of meeting… Sweet Girl was pretty *gut* at driving herself." He chuckled and shook his head. "She could get me to town just fine. The problem came when someone noticed that I had trouble walking from the parking area into the store. In truth, the police had been called because I fell down…"

"Are you okay?" Ada gasped.

Clearly, he was okay, other than being nearly blind.

Clarence patted the air and assured her that he only had a few bumps. "Healed up in no time, but since then, I didn't dare drive. The police were watching for me, though they were nice about it. That officer said he could arrange Handi Rides. I told him I didn't need a Handi Ride, that I had friends."

Someone had strung a rope from the front porch to the barn. Keeping one hand lightly on the rope, he led them to the barn, through it and out the other side to where Sweet Girl was grazing. She was a pretty chestnut mare of medium age and height, and looked to be in *gut* condition.

Ethan checked her teeth, her hooves and her mane. Then he walked her around the pasture. "You've kept her in *gut* shape," he said to the old guy. "I think you'll fetch a fair price for her. Let's take a look at the buggy."

"Won't you miss her something terribly?" Ada asked.

"Oh, for sure and certain I will, but it's important that I think about Sweet Girl and not just my own feelings. She misses trotting down the road, probably gets bored on this farm, if a horse can get bored. *Nein*, it's selfish to keep her. She should be with a family that needs her."

Ada nodded as if she understood, but Ethan thought he saw tears shining in her eyes. He asked her to help him assess the buggy, which had been parked on the other side of the barn.

"Do you really need my help?"

They'd reached the buggy and now she stood in the sunshine, resting against the buggy, head back and face turned up to the sun.

"I wanted to get you away from Clarence before you started crying."

"I wasn't going to cry."

"Could have fooled me."

"What's wrong with crying?"

"Nothing, but it's not typical during a business transaction."

"Humph." Instead of being truly offended, she

opened her eyes and stared out across the pasture. "I was imagining my *dat* being too old to drive."

"Your *dat* is a young man. Clarence is at least thirty years older than him."

"I guess."

Ethan walked around the buggy, trying to keep his attention on it instead of on Ada. He had certainly never met anyone like her. She thought about other people—and other animals—a lot.

Their second stop was to a farm that was technically in a different church district, but it was still close enough to town that the farmer there wanted to sell his pigs at their auction.

Joseph Stoltzfus had forty-two Yorkshire pigs in all, but only eighteen that he was interested in selling. The feeder pigs looked healthy—Stoltzfus had records to show he'd maintained their vaccinations—and Ada was thrilled with the pigpens, fencing and mud wallow.

She was less excited about the smell.

"I had no idea." She practically stuck her head out the open window as they headed back out to the main road.

He couldn't help laughing at her and, rather than becoming defensive, she laughed right along with him.

Ethan thought the morning was going rather well. He was proud of himself for following Sarah's advice. She certainly understood Ada better than he did. He began to feel silly about being so upset around Ada. She wasn't a businessperson, but she also wasn't actively trying to ruin the auction either. She'd simply allowed her imagination to get carried away with fear over some poor animal's situation.

The third farm was another Amish farmer from their church who wanted to sell two geldings. They were in and out from that farm in under thirty minutes.

The last farm they went to was an *Englischer* who had three Holstein dairy cows to sell. Ada said she'd wait by the buggy while Ethan went with the seller to assess the cows. As with the other lots, the animals looked to be healthy. Ethan could only quote what they'd been receiving for dairy cows recently. There was no way to guarantee a certain price, but Mr. Beasley seemed happy with the estimate.

Ethan was congratulating himself on a morning well spent. He shook hands with Mr. Beasley then started back toward his buggy. He hadn't been gone more than twenty minutes, but he knew immediately that something had changed.

Ada was standing beside the buggy, almost as if she needed to protect it. Her arms were crossed and she kept glancing inside as if worried about something.

"What's up?"

"Nothing."

"Huh?"

"Nothing's up."

"It's an expression…like 'how are you doing?'"

"I'm fine, Ethan. How are you?" She darted another glance over her shoulder, and he thought he heard a meow.

He looked under the buggy. No cat.

He turned in a circle. Still no cat. He must have imagined it. "Guess that's it. We're ready to go back to the market, or I could drop you off at home."

"Yeah. That might be better." Now her eyes were wide, expectant, a little worried.

He opened the driver's-side door, hopped in and waited for Ada to do the same. She slowly climbed in next to him.

"This is going to sound crazy," he said, "but I keep hearing a cat."

"Doesn't sound crazy to me."

And then he heard several cats. He turned around and stared into the back seat of his buggy, where he found one cardboard box, one mother cat, and five kittens.

Chapter Eight

Ada's family barely blinked when she showed them the box of kittens.

Sarah found an old blanket to stuff in the box.

"Mr. Beasley's wife was going to take them to the animal shelter. Can you imagine?"

"I can."

"But why put them in a shelter if they can live here…with Ginger and Snap and Pogo and Matilda?"

"Indeed." Eunice looped an arm through Ada's. "Let's go get them settled."

The mother was a calico, which Ada loved. The cat's coat reminded her of a patchwork quilt. Three of the kittens were also calico—smaller versions of the same quilt. One was yellow, and the final one was solid black except for a splash of white between his ears.

Ada was already calling the mother cat

Patches—maybe not an original name, but it fit. Patches hissed when Ginger tried to check out the kittens.

"Too early," Eunice cautioned, picking up the little beagle and snuggling it.

"Whew. It's getting crowded in here."

"It certainly is." Eunice grinned. "Must cost a lot to take care of all these animals."

"That's why I need an organization."

"Ah, yes. The posters. When does this meeting happen?"

"Saturday." Ada stroked a finger along the black kitten's spine. "What if no one shows up?"

"Don't spend your days worrying about what-ifs, sis. You have enough work to keep you busy here without adding that on top."

"Don't I know it." Ada leaned back against the stall's wall. "Say, where is Becca? I wanted to show her the kittens."

"Bed."

"Becca's in bed? In the middle of the day?"

"Headache."

"Oh."

"Gideon's worried it's something more. He has a call in to the doctor."

"Oh!" Ada suddenly felt a need to hug Matilda the donkey. Or maybe Matilda sensed that she needed comfort, because the donkey walked over to her and lay down close enough to press against Ada's side. "Is Sarah worried?"

"Sarah is the first to admit she doesn't know much about pregnant women. That's why Gideon called the doctor."

"Okay."

"Don't worry."

"Jump and let Jesus."

"Whatever." Eunice grinned. "I best get back to my project."

"What are you working on now?"

"Don't laugh."

"I would never."

"A clothes line that…" She held up a finger and moved it in a circle.

"Turns?"

"Exactly."

"Solar-powered," they both said at once then high-fived.

Eunice grinned. "Wind-powered, too, if you think about it."

Ada felt good. She'd spent a nice morning with Ethan, though he'd gone mysteriously silent after seeing the kittens. It could be that he wasn't a cat person. Patches and her five sweet kittens were now snuggling together within the folds of the blanket, inside their box, which she'd placed inside an old crate. Patches could easily jump out, but the kittens were safe as could be. Just as important, Ginger and Snap were too small to climb in.

Matilda completely ignored the kittens and Pogo was worn out from spending the morning in the pasture. The little goat had fallen asleep in the opposite corner of the stall.

Ada thought things were going well. She sat there a few minutes, enjoying her menagerie of animals, thinking that life was good, and she wasn't worried about a single thing.

And then, as abruptly as a northern storm blowing down from the Great Lakes, things took a dramatic turn toward trouble.

Gideon and their youngest mare Kit Kat arrived in a flurry. She'd only seen anyone drive a horse that fast when they had buggy races. Why would Gideon be racing Kit Kat? The horse didn't seem to mind, tossing her head as Gideon set the brake and jumped out of the buggy.

"What's going on?" Ada ran to catch up with Gideon and follow him inside. He hadn't even spoken to her, hadn't seemed to notice she was there at his heels. Instead, he'd hurried into the house and dashed up the stairs where Becca had been resting in her old room.

"What's happening?" She turned in a circle and sighed with relief when Eunice walked down the stairs and into the room. Eunice always understood what was happening. "Is everyone all right?"

"The doctor wants to see Becca," Eunice explained. "They're just being extra careful since this is her first *boppli*."

Becca made it to the bottom of the stairs, Gideon hovering at her elbow.

Ada suddenly felt like crying. It wasn't supposed to happen this way. Pregnancy was supposed to be a happy time where you kept your feet propped up and your family waited on you. She hated this. She hated the looks of worry on everyone's faces.

Eunice perched on the edge of a chair. "Are you okay, sis?"

"*Ya*. Just…" She shook her head and closed her eyes. "Just a headache is all."

"Your feet sure are swollen," Ada blurted out.

Becca reached out and put a hand against the wall.

"What is it?" Gideon asked.

"Dizzy…a little."

Sarah bustled across the room. "I've packed a bag for you to take with you to the doctor, just in case she wants to put you into the hospital."

"Hospital?" Ada looked at Eunice, who shrugged.

"Let's get you to the buggy," Gideon said.

They all followed her out, hovering, worrying,

and then—once Gideon and Becca were headed down the road—praying.

When her *dat* came home, he told them that the doctor had decided to admit Becca. He'd stopped by and updated Bethany and Aaron. Gideon would spend the night at the hospital.

The dinner meal was a somber affair. Ada couldn't think of a single misquote that might make her family smile. She couldn't think of anything except for the look of worry on Gideon's face and the look of discomfort on Becca's.

They all agreed it would be best to go to bed early, but first they needed to talk to Gideon on their *dat*'s emergency phone. They stepped outside to call him, which seemed silly to Ada. What difference did it matter if the phone was in the house or outside? She wanted to know how her *schweschder* was feeling and how her *boppli* was doing.

"It's the idea of the thing," Sarah had explained to her more than once. "We don't want people on the phone in the kitchen or the sitting room…that's where we talk to each other. That's where we're a family."

They stood together on the front porch. Eunice had figured out how to push one of the buttons so they could all hear. Their *dat* assured them that there was a phone in Becca's hospital room, and Gideon picked up on the second ring.

He didn't know much else about Becca's condition, but she was resting and seemed a tad more comfortable.

Eunice closed her eyes and said, "We love you, sis."

"We're praying," Ada's *dat* assured her.

Sarah, as always, was practical. "Make sure they feed you well."

But, for Ada, her words stuck in her throat. She wanted to say a dozen different things. She wanted to mess up some saying and make everyone laugh. She wanted things to be as they were before Gideon had raced into the yard. The words threatened to catch in her throat, but she managed to croak, "Come home quick."

Ada thought she wouldn't sleep. She missed Becca and she missed Bethany, and she didn't understand why life had to be hard. She thought she would stay awake worrying about those things, but instead she dropped off nearly as soon as she lay down.

It seemed only a few minutes later she found herself blinking at the soft light coming through her window as Sarah bustled around, telling her it was time to get up. "Family meeting during breakfast. Best get hopping."

Ethan noticed immediately that something was wrong with Ada. She was the kind of person who didn't try to hide her feelings. He saw, etched on her face, sadness and depression, and worry.

"What is it?"

She told him about Becca, told him that her *schweschder* had spent the night in the hospital and was going to spend another night.

"Amos stopped by last night and told us," he said. "We all prayed for her. I'm sure she's going to be fine."

"I need to see her, but instead I'm here at this auction."

"Couldn't you—"

She shook her head. "*Dat* said it would be best to carry on, and that there was nothing we could do there."

"He's right, of course. But still, it's understandable that you would want to see her."

"Sarah and Eunice hired a driver and went this morning. I'm going to go with *Dat* tonight. It just seems…well a long time away." She stared at her clipboard and pulled in her bottom lip.

"I'm sorry, Ada. Please let me know if there's anything I can do."

Ada nodded, turned and walked away.

Ethan asked around and it seemed that whatever was ailing Becca wasn't too terribly serious. The Amish grapevine was working well. Everyone had heard about the emergency trip to the hospital. The fact that Gideon was their assistant manager, Amos was their general manager, and Becca had once worked at the auction, made them seem like family to all of the employees.

Ethan heard things like, "She got there in plenty of time," and "The *boppli*'s heartbeat is strong." It all sounded very hopeful to him. He could understand why Ada was upset though. Becca's condition had apparently surprised everyone. He'd seen her the week before helping Gideon in the office, and she'd seemed fine!

Life could turn on a dime.

He smiled to himself. Ada wouldn't have said it that way. Life could turn on a nickel? Life could turn upside down? Life could turn on a lemon slice? Yeah, that sounded like Ada.

The horse auction that morning went off without a hitch.

At lunch, he went in search of Ada. When he found her, he suggested they go to JoJo's for a pretzel.

"I'm not very hungry."

"But you'll be having a late dinner since you're going to the hospital with your *dat*. You'll be glad you stopped to have lunch."

"Okay. *Ya. Gut* idea."

She didn't talk a lot as they walked toward Davis Mercantile, where JoJo's Pretzels was located. The day was overcast and cool, but there wasn't any rain or snow falling. To Ethan, it seemed like a pretty typical October day in northern Indiana. In fact, October was nearly over. November was around the corner and beyond that was Christmas, which was always busy at the market.

To Ethan, it all seemed like just one more thing.

On top of all the other things.

He couldn't get excited about any of it.

Ada, though… Ada saw things through fresh eyes. She stopped to looked at the pumpkin display in a shop window, waved at a small *Englisch* toddler, picked up a piece of trash on the sidewalk and tossed it into a receptacle.

By the time they were seated in the coffee shop adjacent to JoJo's, enjoying fresh coffee and their pretzels—his, original, hers, cinnamon and sugar—she seemed ready to talk.

"Tell me what you know about Becca's condition."

"Oh, *ya*. I guess you saw *Dat* come over and talk to me during the auction. Honestly, it was the one moment I had forgotten about Becca because Clarence's mare was up for sale."

"Zeb Mast bought him."

"Zeb takes very *gut* care of his horses." She nibbled around a corner of her pretzel.

"So, about Becca…"

"Right. So, Becca is pretty far along in her pregnancy. Her *boppli* is due just after Christmas."

"And Bethany is due the week before."

"Exactly. By the first of the year, we're going to have a full bowl."

"Full plate?"

"Maybe. So, anyway…" She took a large bite of her pretzel and swigged it down with coffee… coffee topped with whipped cream and orange sprinkles, which she had smiled at enormously when the girl behind the counter had handed it to her. "Becca has been experiencing terrible headaches and swelling and dizziness. Turns out the cause is high blood pressure."

"Oh."

"Exactly. Lots of old folks have that, right? Turns out, with a pregnant mom, it can be a big thing."

He shifted uncomfortably in his seat and added Becca's blood pressure to his mental list of things he should worry about. And Bethany. What if she had it, too, and didn't know it?

"How big a thing?"

"Very, if you don't catch it in time." Ada took another sip of her coffee and managed to leave a good portion of the whipped cream on her upper lip.

Without thinking, Ethan leaned forward and wiped it off with his thumb.

"Oh. *Danki.*"

"Gem gschehne."

She seemed to lose her train of thought, shook her head, and then took another bite of the pretzel. "The doctor is concerned about Becca because high blood pressure can lead to something called preeclampsia, which could cause her to go into labor early or it could even cause her to have a seizure."

"But she caught it in time."

"Ya. Becca doesn't have preeclampsia yet, or if she does, it's mild. So the doctor is sending her home tomorrow."

"That's awesome."

"She's to stay in bed as much as possible, lying on her left side if she can, though I can't imagine why it would matter which side you're lying on."

Ethan shook his head. It was all a lot to take in. He probably wasn't ready to be married. There was more to having babies than he'd ever considered.

"She'll take some medicine, have weekly visits from the home health nurse…" She finished her pretzel, drained her cup of coffee, and smiled. "We had a family meeting this morning."

"Ya?"

"Looks like we'll be having another tonight."

"That's *gut.* It's *wunderbaar* that you're all there to help Gideon and Becca."

"And you're there to help Aaron and Bethany."

He nodded. It was nice to have someone acknowledge that. They were all family. They would help one another, but they each had their own part to do. Maybe he should just focus on his part.

As if reading his mind, Ada said, "My job will be to bring Becca books and magazines from the library so she doesn't get bored. I'm also to help her write her letters. She writes every week to the people she helped on her Mennonite Disaster Service missions. They're like... pencil pals now."

He didn't correct that one.

Pencil pals sounded every bit as *gut* as pen pals.

They bussed their table then walked slowly back to the market. For once, Ethan's mind was not whirling with thoughts of all the things he needed to do, all of the things he needed to worry about. Instead, he found himself laughing with Ada as they counted scarecrows...there were twenty-three.

Twenty-three scarecrows between JoJo's Pretzels and the market. He would never have guessed. He would never have noticed if it wasn't for the woman walking by his side.

And then, as they rounded the corner of the auction building, still out of sight of the other employees, the strangest thing happened. Ada stopped to stare at a chalk drawing of a pumpkin on the ground...something done by a child, no doubt, since the pumpkin was oddly shaped and purple rather than orange.

He didn't notice that right away though.

Ada had stopped quite suddenly to avoid stepping on the chalk drawing.

Ethan nearly ran into her, but at the last second, he put out his arms to keep from knocking her down. Ada turned, regained her balance, and somehow there was no space between them. She was literally standing in the circle of his arms.

So Ethan did what any man would naturally do when holding a beautiful woman.

He kissed her.

Chapter Nine

Ethan tried not to think of that kiss. He pushed it out of his mind the rest of the day and on the ride home, and even through dinner. But once he was in the barn that night, seeing to the horses, he couldn't help replaying the moment.

She had seemed so surprised.

But she had definitely leaned into the kiss.

He was sure that she had.

Then they'd both jumped back as if they'd received an electrical shock. He'd apologized, and she'd said no, it was her fault, and they'd walked the rest of the way to the market in an awkward silence then bustled off in opposite directions.

He had kissed Ada Yoder.

Why had he done such a thing?

He'd kissed girls before. Of course, he had. There was the girl in eighth grade who'd had a gap between her front teeth and freckles across the bridge of her nose. What was her name?

There was also Abbey, the *Englisch* girl in Ohio, whom he'd been fascinated with for the better part of a year. He'd kissed her several times, then she'd gone off to college in Texas, and that had been the end of that.

He was sure there were more women he'd kissed—women he'd been interested in—but he couldn't think of them. All he could think of was Ada.

He groaned at the thought of the huge mistake he'd made. He'd let his instincts, his feelings, get the best of him. Now things were going to be weird between them.

Unless they weren't.

He supposed that was a possibility, even if it was a slim one.

He tossed that idea back and forth, wondering if what he was thinking was a brilliant or colossally stupid thing to think. Could he date Ada Yoder? Would she be interested in him?

Misty had no answers. She nodded her head as he brushed her mane. Dixie stomped her right front hoof, but he didn't think that was a vote for or against his plan. Was it a plan?

He was turning it over and over in his mind as he closed up the barn and then he heard the front door slam.

Aaron shouted, "Ethan, we need you."

There was such desperation and fear in his

bruder's voice that at first Aaron thought he must be playing a joke. Could anyone become that distressed in the space of an hour? They'd just all had dinner together.

He jogged toward the front porch.

One glance at Aaron's face told him this was no joke.

"Beth is bleeding. Run to the phone booth. Call an ambulance."

"Okay. Sure." He didn't turn back, didn't ask any questions, simply ran as fast as he could into the darkness. The nearest phone booth was only a quarter of a mile down the road. He placed the emergency call, made sure they had the correct address, then ran back to the farm.

As he hurried down the lane, he noticed that bright lantern light spilled from every window.

He hustled up the porch steps. "They'll be here any minute."

Bethany was lying on the couch and smiling weakly. "Thanks, Ethan."

"Of course. You just…just rest."

She looked pale and scared. She looked a lot like Ada, and when he thought of that, a new grief tore through his heart. Ada had been so worried about Becca, and now this. It seemed like too much. It seemed like a very bad dream. And then he noticed the thin trail of blood leading from the bedroom to the couch. His heart beat faster and his palms began to sweat, and he wondered what was taking that ambulance so long.

Aaron walked into the room, carrying a canvas bag.

"Did you get my nightgown?"

"Ya."

"And..." She glanced at Ethan, then back at her husband and shook her head as if she couldn't believe what she was about to say. "My underthings?"

"Ya. I got it all."

"And the knitting?"

"I got the knitting, but Beth..."

"And my Bible."

"Ya."

The scream of a siren split the night and then everything happened very fast. The ambulance came to a stop right in front of the house. Two paramedics...one young woman whose name tag said Vicki and an older man whose name tag said Grant...hustled into the room as if they'd done this a thousand times, and maybe they had. Ethan prayed they had and that they knew exactly what they were doing.

"I'm Aaron, and this is my *fraa*, Bethany."

"I'm in my third trimester," Beth said softly.

The woman knelt next to the couch and fastened a blood pressure cuff around Beth's arm. "Bethany, I want you to try and breath slowly.

While I take your pressure, Aaron can tell me what happened."

"I was doing up the dinner dishes—"

"Good man," Vicki teased in a low voice and Bethany smiled.

Surely, if the woman could joke around then this wasn't as serious as it looked.

"Then Bethany called out and I walked into the bathroom and saw her standing there...bleeding."

"Can you tell me how much blood there was?"

He looked at her blankly.

"Teaspoonful or cupful?"

"Something in between."

Ethan nearly fell over at that—she'd lost half a cup of blood? That was a lot, wasn't it? Why weren't they giving her a transfusion this very minute?

As Vicki worked and asked questions, the older paramedic called in an update to the hospital. "Our ETA is twenty minutes." They both helped Bethany onto a stretcher and rolled her out to the ambulance.

Vicki poked her head out the bay doors of the vehicle. "Climb in with me, Aaron. I'm sure your wife will feel better if you ride along."

Aaron glanced at Ethan then, who said, "Go. Go with her. I'll see to everything here and then call a driver."

Aaron climbed into the back of the ambulance

with Vicki and Bethany. Grant slapped the doors shut. He opened the driver's-side door, hopped in and then rolled down his window. "We're taking her to Goshen Health. Do you know where that is?"

"I'll find it."

There was the blip of the siren, the lights throwing bars of red across the fields, and then they were gone.

And Ethan was left, wondering how his world had turned upside down, and how he'd possibly thought he'd had problems before. He hadn't had any real problems. He'd had problems that he'd created out of thin air.

Adding on an extra room?

Worrying about next year's rain?

Kissing a girl?

Those things were so trivial. What mattered was family. What mattered was taking care of each other, and Ethan vowed in that very minute that he would stay focused on the important things. And he would remember to be grateful. *Just let her be okay,* Gotte. *Let the* boppli *be fine.* The prayer was more than just words muttered under his breath. The prayer was from the deepest part of his heart.

The Yoder family was sitting in the living room when Ethan called. Ada had been to the hospital with her *dat*. It had helped ease her worries to see Becca smiling, to see her acting like her old self. If she continued to improve, she'd be able to come home the next day.

Then her *dat*'s emergency phone rang.

It was Ethan.

Something was terribly wrong.

Ada could only hear her *dat*'s side of the conversation, but it was definitely about Bethany. She was at the hospital. Ethan would call them with updates. If Ethan had thought that their family was going to be satisfied with updates over the phone, he was mistaken. They'd stayed home when Becca had first gone to the hospital because Becca and Gideon had both insisted. Also because Becca had needed to rest. This was different. This was a whole other kind of emergency.

Forty-five minutes after the phone call, they had contacted the driver who had just brought them home, and he'd agreed to take them back over to Goshen.

They all packed into the van and Ada thought that there was some comfort in being bunched between Sarah and Eunice on the seat. There was a sweet consolation in going through this together. They were a family. They would be there for one another. Wasn't that what she and Ethan had just been talking about? And then he'd kissed her.

He'd kissed her.

She pushed that memory from her mind. She could not think about that right now. She had to think about Bethany and Becca and the *bopplin*.

After what felt like an interminably long ride—much longer than the recent ride home along the same road to and from the same places—they arrived at the hospital and rushed into the waiting room.

"Aaron's back with her," Ethan said. "And Ezekiel is on his way."

"*Gut*. That's *gut*." Amos motioned to a corner of the waiting room. Though the other seats were empty at the moment, the corner gave the illusion of being at home. They pulled a few chairs over to make a circle and then Amos reached for Sarah's hand, Sarah reached for Eunice's, Eunice reached for Ada's and Ada reached for Ethan's.

Ethan stepped into the circle as if he belonged there.

Everyone bowed their head as Amos began to pray.

"*Gotte*, Our Father, we trust Bethany and her child to Your care as we trust Becca and her child. We ask You to bless the doctors and nurses, to calm our hearts and the hearts of Gideon and Aaron. Give us courage where we'll need it, patience as we wait, and grace through all things…"

The word "amen" flowed around the circle.

Ada snuck a glance at Ethan as she dropped his hand. "Are you okay?"

"I guess. It was…it was pretty intense."

"Everything is going to be fine, Ethan. You didn't drop the racquet here."

"Huh?"

"She means 'drop the ball,' and Ada's right." Eunice flopped into a chair and picked up a magazine from the side table, but she didn't open it. She simply stared at the cover. "This isn't your fault or anyone else's. This is what they call trying times. Everyone goes through them."

Eunice sighed the sigh of a much older person.

Ada perched on the chair next to Ethan, wondering what could possibly happen next. It seemed like her family was falling apart, but she refused to believe that. It felt like a new disaster popped up every few moments.

Would the ceiling fall in on her head next?

Possibly an early blizzard would trap them in the hospital.

Or she could come down with the measles. What if she had them already? What if she'd exposed everyone?

"I need to walk." She popped up and was halfway across the room before she realized that Ethan was with her.

"Sarah thought I should keep you company."

"Okay."

"Where are we going?"

"I have no idea."

It turned out the corridor made a sort of circle through the facility. They plodded past the closed cafeteria, past the vending machines, past the window that peeked in on the new babies. Ada didn't dare look in that window. She'd start crying for sure and certain if she did. Better to stare straight ahead and keep walking. They were finishing their third lap when a doctor stepped into the waiting room and headed toward her *dat*. Ada and Ethan made a beeline to catch up. They arrived as the doctor was saying, "Well, it's nice to see you all again, though, of course, the reason for seeing you isn't what any of us would wish for."

Gideon had joined the group. He offered Ada a small wave then turned his attention to the doctor.

"Same doctor that Becca has," Ada whispered in response to Ethan's questioning look.

"Let's talk." The doctor's name was Tam Nguyen and she had a pleasant though serious nature about her. "First, I want you to know that Bethany has stabilized and the baby is fine."

Ada's knees felt suddenly weak.

She must have stumbled back a little because Ethan nudged her toward a chair. "You should sit," he whispered. When she did, he stood behind her, hands on the back of the chair.

"Bethany has a condition caused placenta previa. It's basically where the placenta is low in the uterus." The doctor was holding a tablet. She began tapping on its screen until she found the graph she wanted. It showed a baby lying upside down in a bubble—in a uterus, as it was plainly labeled.

"In Bethany's situation, the placenta is only partially covering the cervix."

"That's *gut*?" Amos asked.

"It is. I'm not going to sugar-coat this. It can be serious, and in some cases it requires an emergency C-section. In nine out of ten cases, though, the situation will resolve on its own."

Sarah was nodding, but she looked worried. "Will she be on bedrest? Like Becca?"

"No. In these situations, complete bed rest could increase the risk of blood clots. Instead, we'll restrict her activity…no hanging clothes on the line or carrying anything over five pounds, and I'd like someone to be with her at all times."

"Aaron and Ethan are there with her," Amos said.

"*Ya*, we live together in my parents' home." Ethan cleared his throat and tried to sound more confident than he felt. "Aaron and I are there every morning, every night, and on weekends, too, of course."

Now the doctor turned her attention to him. "You live on a farm?"

"*Ya.* Just outside Shipshe."

"No cell phone?"

"*Nein.*"

"Would your bishop allow one?"

"I most certainly would." Ezekiel smiled as he joined the group. "Sorry I'm late. Had a little trouble finding a driver. I would certainly allow for Bethany to have a phone in her home if it's medically necessary."

"It is," the doctor assured him.

"I'll pick one up tomorrow," Amos said.

The doctor smiled then continued. "I'd also prefer that someone is with her at all times. We don't want her bleeding to start again and her be on the farm alone—even with the phone, it might be in the other room, or she might have trouble getting a signal. Someone should be there, if that's at all possible."

"It's possible," Sarah assured her. "We'll work it out."

Dr. Nguyen stood and studied the group. "The next two months may require a lot from each of you, but by the time we ring in the new year, you'll have two healthy babies."

After she'd walked out of the waiting area

and back through the double doors that led to the emergency ward, everyone started talking at once. After a few minutes of that, Ada's *dat* raised his hand to quiet them. "Family meeting?"

"Ya," Ezekiel agreed. "Family meeting."

Amos waited until everyone was seated—including Gideon, Ethan and the bishop. "As the doctor said, the next two months will require a lot from each of you, but we have a strong family. We will get through this."

Tears pricked Ada's eyes and she blinked furiously to prevent them from falling. She would not cry. She wasn't the one hurting here—Becca and Bethany were.

"Someone needs to stay with Bethany," Sarah said. "That seems to be the most pressing issue."

"But... Aaron and I are there." Ethan shook his head, not comprehending what she was suggesting. "Maybe one of us could stay home mornings and the other in the afternoon..."

He didn't seem to comprehend what the doctor had said.

But Ada understood. "One of us. One of us needs to stay with her."

"Exactly," Sarah agreed. "Help with the cooking and cleaning, be there during the day while Aaron and Ethan are at work."

"I'll go." The words popped out of Ada's mouth. She couldn't have explained why she'd volunteered, why it was suddenly so important to her to be the one staying with Bethany. She'd been rescuing animals for nearly a month, and it had taught her a lot. Mostly, it had taught her that she could do a thing if she set her mind to it, and she could do this.

Sarah and Eunice were looking at her in surprise.

Amos was combing his fingers through his beard.

It was Ezekiel who sealed the deal. "I think it's a *wunderbaar* idea. Ada will stay at the King farm. Sarah and Eunice will stay at the Yoder farm. Amos, Ethan, Aaron and Gideon can continue to work at the market…though if you need a break, if you need anything, our church members will be willing to step in."

Amos started to say something but Ezekiel stopped him with a small shake of his head. Ada had never seen anyone stop her *dat* before. It was an odd thing to witness.

"Accepting help is important, Amos. I don't mean only monetary help. I understand that you are blessed in that way, and your generosity when others have been in need has reflected that blessing. But I suspect that, in this current situation, there will be other things you will need. Help can come in many shapes and forms. It will be up to you to let me know when and where it's needed."

Amos nodded in appreciation, then said, "*Ya.* Of course, you are right, Ezekiel. *Danki.*"

"*Gem gschehne.*"

Ada didn't even notice that Ethan had become quite still…and completely silent. Gideon left to update Becca, Sarah and Eunice went to fetch coffee and snacks, and Ezekiel went through the double doors to pray with Bethany.

All that was left in the corner of the waiting room was Amos, Ethan and Ada. Ethan coughed then said, "Amos, if I could, I'd like to speak with you privately."

Amos studied him then Ada. Finally, he said, "We're family, Ethan. Whatever you have to say…you can say in front of Ada."

What wouldn't he want to say in front of her?

Why did he have that sour look on his face again?

"All right. It's only that I'm worried about this arrangement."

"'Arrangement'?"

"I'm concerned about having Ada stay at our home. I assume you mean she would be there day and night."

"Yes, that would probably be best. We want someone with Bethany at all times, and you know as well as I do…life on a farm often causes you to be out of the home at odd hours and for a dozen different reasons."

"I understand, but...we only have the two bedrooms." His face colored as he tossed another glance at Ada. "The house is quite small."

Amos laughed for the first time that evening. "Do you remember when you and Aaron stayed with us? After your house had nearly burned to the ground?"

"I remember."

"Four girls in one room. Isn't that right, Ada?"

"*Ya.* I thought it would be the best sleepover ever, but then I realized being packed in like shrimp..."

"Sardines?"

"That it wasn't easy. A couple of times I considered going out to the barn just to have a little privacy."

"But you all survived. You survived and you became closer as *schweschdern. Gotte* used that experience for your blessing, *ya*?"

"*Ya.*" Thinking back on those days when she could not wait to have a little time alone again, Ada understood that she'd taken many things for granted. She'd taken her *schweschdern* for granted. She'd taken her family's health for granted. She'd even taken the simplicity of the times for granted.

Her *dat* stood and adjusted his suspenders, his gaze on something outside the windows, though he was plainly still addressing Ada and Ethan.

"You two have come a long way from the day that you came into my office worried about a litter of beagles. You've learned to work together."

Ada thought that was true.

She thought of visiting the farms with Ethan. Had that really been the day before? It seemed like a lifetime ago.

She remembered the kiss.

Ethan didn't look like he wanted to kiss her now. He was still frowning, still looking sour as an old green apple, but he nodded in agreement with Amos.

Standing, Ethan muttered, "Think I could use some fresh air," and he walked out of the room, leaving her sitting there, wondering what had just happened.

Why had she volunteered in the first place? Plainly, Ethan would be more comfortable with someone else...with anyone else. Sarah could have gone. Or Eunice. Why had she jumped up and thrown her name in the circle?

But she had, and there was no turning back.

She'd do whatever she needed to do to support Bethany.

And Ethan was going to have to deal with it.

Chapter Ten

On Saturday at five minutes until noon, Ethan found himself sitting at JoJo's Pretzels. Taped to the front of the table where he was sitting was a sign that read Amish for the Humane Treatment of Auction Animals. Fortunately—or maybe unfortunately—no one had shown up for Ada's meeting yet.

Then a gray-haired woman walked over to the table. "Mind if I sit?"

"Um, sure. I guess. *Ya.*"

When he didn't say anything else, she glanced at her watch. "I guess we're it."

"We're it?"

She pointed to the poster.

"Oh. You're here for the meeting!"

"Indeed."

Ethan took a big breath. Ada had gone over and over what he was supposed to say. He could do this.

"My name is Sally Drummond." She waited, and he finally realized he was supposed to introduce himself.

"I'm Ethan. Ethan King."

She smiled as if she'd known all along that he was capable of remembering his own name, and then she tapped the table. "I think I'll grab a pretzel and a coffee. Can I get you anything?"

"*Nein.* I'm *gut.*" He'd already consumed two cups of strong coffee and a cinnamon pretzel. The combination of sugar and caffeine was making him a bit nauseous.

"Right back, then, and you can tell me all about your organization."

He wanted to shout that it wasn't his organization at all, but that seemed inappropriate as she walked away. So, instead, he sat there and fervently hoped no one else would show up. He didn't like speaking to crowds. On the other hand, he rather hoped someone would show up, because he did not look forward to telling Ada that her organizational meeting had been a bust.

When Sally Drummond returned, Ethan again became a bit tongue-tied. Rather than be surprised by that, Sally sipped her coffee and waited.

"This isn't my organization," he finally blurted out.

"Okay."

"It's my friend's…" Was Ada his friend? Why

had he kissed her? And what was he going to be about her living in his house?

"Your friend is…"

"Ada. Ada Yoder."

Sally seemed to be considering that as she sipped her coffee. Finally, she asked, "Is she a young Amish girl? Blond hair, blue eyes, lots of energy?"

"*Ya*. That would be Ada."

"I think she picked up a flyer from our table—the SPCA table."

"SPCA?"

"Society for the Prevention of Cruelty to Animals. We had an information booth set up during the music festival in the park."

"Maybe so. She did go to that."

"Okay. So where is Ada today?" Sally had chosen a whole-wheat pretzel and proceeded to cover it with Amish-made natural peanut butter. Satisfied that she had it exactly as she liked, Sally broke off a piece of her pretzel, chewed a moment, then washed it down with coffee. Obviously, she was waiting for Ethan to untie his tongue.

"Ada's moving today."

"Moving?" Sally's eyebrows arched. "Funny time to start a new organization."

"Oh, she's not moving far. See…her *schweschder* Bethany is married to my *bruder* Aaron. She's expecting—"

"Bethany is?"

"Right, and she's…well, she's having trouble carrying the baby. Ada is moving into our place so someone can be there with Bethany all the time."

"Ah. I see." She glanced again at the sheet of paper taped to the table, pronouncing the name of Ada's group. "'Amish for the Humane Treatment of Auction Animals.' Tell me about why Ada thinks there needs to be an Amish group that is overseeing the treatment of auction animals."

"What do you mean?"

"Well, why Amish? Why not everyone?"

"*Ya. Gut* point."

"And why auction animals in particular? Of course, there are regulations in place, and I have personally never fielded a call of any problem at our local auction. I assume you know the one here in town."

"Yes. It's where I work."

"The plot thickens."

Ethan wasn't sure what that meant, but the woman's relaxed posture was taking the edge off his nerves. He found himself explaining to her about the litter of beagle pups Ada had rescued, and then the young goat, the blind donkey and, finally, the kittens.

"Wow. Your Ada sounds like quite the girl."

"Not my Ada, but *ya*…she's something else for certain."

Sally sat back and studied him. Finally, she said, "I admire what she's trying to do, but maybe she doesn't have to recreate the whole process."

"What do you mean?"

"Well, at our chapter of the SPCA we have a budget, we have followers and supporters, and we have visibility."

Ethan didn't know what to say to that, so he didn't say anything. But, Sally, she looked as if she'd landed on an idea that she liked very much.

"Ada could speak to our people. We have a group meeting once a month."

"She's pretty busy right now."

"Because she's moving. Because of her sister."

"Right."

Sally finished her coffee, wadded up the little bag the pretzel came in, and carried both over to the trash can. When she came back to the table, she was smiling. She reached into her purse, pulled out a card, found a pen and scribbled a note on the back. Handing it to Ethan, she said, "Give this to her for me?"

"Sure. *Ya.*"

"It was nice to meet you."

"And you as well."

Sally walked away and Ethan glanced at his watch, surprised to see that it was twelve thirty. He'd waited an appropriate amount of time. Ada wouldn't expect him to stay any longer. He bussed the table then glanced at the business card Sally had left with him.

SPCA
Society for Prevention of Cruelty to Animals
Sally Drummond

That was followed by a web page and a phone number. There was the outlined image of a cat and a dog on the bottom left-and right-hand corners. He turned the card over and read the message Sally had written.

Ada, call me.
I think we can help each other.

It didn't make much sense to Ethan. He almost threw the card away, but then it occurred to him that maybe it would make more sense to Ada. Or maybe she'd want to call the woman and talk to her. He stuck the card in his pocket and hurried out onto the street. A light rain had begun to fall and it was colder now than it had been when he'd set out that morning.

Not the best conditions for Ada's impending move.

But then, she wasn't really moving. She was relocating for a few weeks. Okay, for two months. Bethany was on board with it. Aaron seemed satisfied. Ethan realized he needed to put aside his reservations, figure out how he could help, and forget about that kiss.

The first two things might be doable, but he didn't think the last one was going to happen. Ada would be sitting at their table for breakfast, lunch and dinner. He wasn't always home for lunch, but that wasn't the point. Ada would be in the living room, in the kitchen, and staying in his bedroom.

She'd have no need to be in the barn.

Perhaps he could take up residence out there.

Surely, the twenty yards between the house and the barn would be enough distance to allow him to keep his feelings for her at bay.

Ada didn't pack very much for her move to Bethany's. What did she need besides her clothes? She wanted to take the animals, but Sarah nixed the idea.

"Eunice will look after your animals."

"I'm happy to do it," Eunice confirmed as she walked through the kitchen to the mudroom and outside. Eunice didn't seem at all concerned by the cold weather and rain. She took things in stride.

Ada would like to be more like that, but she had no idea how. Things…even small things like the weather…could affect her mood in big ways. And big things—like illness and moving—could set her adrift completely. She glanced around the kitchen as she sat down to her now-cold mug of coffee.

"Want me to freshen that up?" Sarah asked, not even turning around from the sink.

How did she know that Ada was thinking about coffee? Sarah was scary sometimes.

"Nein." She sighed heavily. "Probably wouldn't help."

Their *dat* had left early for the market, taking care of a few things he'd let slide due to the dual health emergencies. Becca and Bethany were to be released from the hospital, and would be sharing a ride home along with Gideon and Aaron.

"I spoke to *dat* earlier this morning," Sarah said, turning to look at her. "We're going to be moving his things up to Becca and Gideon's room…and their things down to his room."

"Why would we do that? I guess I can see why they'd move back into our house, but…" Ada sat back, crossing her arms and frowning at her *schweschder*. It seemed the entire world was going mad. Why was everything changing?

Sarah smiled at Ada's glum expression. She wiped her hands with a dishtowel and sat at the table. "What's it to you, kid?"

Ada couldn't help smiling at that. Sarah sounded funny when she tried to talk *Englisch*. Her smile didn't last though. This wasn't funny.

Life was not at all funny right now. "I just don't see why everything has to change."

"Give me a for instance."

"*Dat* changing rooms."

"We think it would be better if Becca didn't have to go up and down the stairs."

"Oh. Right. That makes sense."

"What else is bothering you?"

"I don't like leaving my animals. Ginger and Snap get bigger every day. I'm going to miss their puppy years...days...whatever. Matilda has just learned to find her way from the pasture to the barn. Pogo, as you know, is always finding trouble. And the kittens are still so small! I'm going to miss their baby days."

"We all have to make sacrifices, Ada. I know you understand that."

Ada nodded but she didn't speak. Now tears were pooling in her eyes and she did her best to blink them away. Crying was something a *boppli* did. She was an adult. It was time she started to act like one. "Right. You're right."

"We'll make sure you get over here at least twice a week to spend time with your animals."

"*Ya?*"

"Sure. It's the least we can do." Sarah reached forward and tucked an errant hair behind Ada's ear. "Plus, that way you can clean up the stall where you're housing all those orphaned animals."

"It's not that many…only two dogs, a goat, a donkey, one cat and five kittens." Ada did laugh when Sarah ducked her head and gave her the look. "All right. It's kind of a lot."

"Are you going to miss working at the auction?"

"Not really," Ada admitted. "It was exciting at first. I felt useful. I thought I was saving animals, but in truth…not that many animals needed saving."

"Don't sell yourself short. *Dat* told me you added a much-needed perspective."

"He said that?"

"He did."

Ada sat straighter then she remembered about her organizational meeting. "I can't believe that Ethan had to fill in for me at the pretzel shop."

"Well, he couldn't very well pack your clothes."

"True."

"I'm sure he did a *gut* job."

"I guess." Ada wasn't at all sure about that though. Ethan was tolerating her, but he didn't understand her. He certainly didn't understand how she felt about animals.

Sarah sat back and studied her. Finally, she asked, "Is there something you want to talk about? Maybe something in regard to Ethan?"

"He kissed me," Ada blurted out then covered her mouth with her hand. "Oops. I let the racoon out of the bag."

"Cat. You let the cat out of the bag."

"Who would put a cat in a bag?"

"Tell me about the kiss."

So, she did. She told about going to have a pretzel with Ethan, about how he was suddenly kind and attentive, and about the kiss. Then she followed it with a question. "But did you see his reaction at the hospital last night? He was not happy to hear that I was moving in with him."

"Maybe he's embarrassed."

"Embarrassed? What does he have to be embarrassed about?"

"Their house is smaller, some might say poorer."

"I don't care about that."

"I know you don't. You're a *gut* person, Ada Yoder."

That made Ada feel inexplicably better. "I can move *Dat*'s clothes."

"That would be very helpful."

They spent the next hour swapping the items in both bedrooms. By the time Gideon and Becca pulled up, everything was ready. It was a *gut* thing, too, as one look at Becca told Ada that she needed a nap, and she most certainly did not need to climb the stairs.

She went in to see her before she left for Bethany's.

Becca was sitting up, pillows propped behind

her, and all the supplies for her letter writing spread around her.

"Shouldn't you be napping?"

"I'm resting. It's practically the same thing." She patted the side of the bed. "Sit down and tell me about moving to Beth's."

So, Ada did. She told her about her initial conflict with Ethan all the way up to the kiss. She told her how oddly he'd acted the night before, and she shared Sarah's idea about why he might have done that.

"It could be that he's embarrassed." Becca laid a hand on her stomach then smiled at Ada. "When we went to help people with MDS, they were often embarrassed about their homes or their yards. I'd try to put them at ease by commenting on their clothesline and telling them about ours."

"And did it work? Did it put them at ease?"

"Sometimes. Other times it just took being around them for a few days before they truly believed that we weren't judging them."

"You're telling me to be patient." Ada rolled her eyes. "As I'm sure you're aware, that doesn't come naturally for me."

"You can do it though. I believe in you."

"*Danki*, but we all know that giraffes don't change their stripes very often."

"Zebras. The saying is zebras don't change their stripes."

Ada didn't care if Becca corrected her. Becca was smiling, and that was what mattered. "Take care of my niece or nephew."

Becca's smile widened.

"What?"

"I didn't say anything."

"When I said… Oh, my. You know? You know if it's a girl or boy?"

Becca nodded her head. "They had to do a sonogram to make sure everything was okay, and it was…well, it was obvious to the technician."

"Don't tell me." Ada clapped her hands over her ears. That lasted about three seconds. "Tell me."

Twenty minutes later, her *dat* was back and ready to take her to Bethany's. She'd already said goodbye to her *schweschdern* and her sweet animals. In fact, she was sitting on the porch, her bag packed beside her, ready to go.

If her *dat* was surprised at her punctuality, he didn't show it. Instead, he nodded as if it was what he'd expected, and she loved him for that.

On the way to Huckleberry Lane, he did remind her of why she was moving there. "You're to help Bethany in every way you can."

"Of course, but…give me some examples. I know the doctor said she wasn't to stay in bed all the time, but what can she do?"

"She can go on short walks, but only if someone is with her."

"I can do that."

"She can go outside with you to hang up the laundry, but you're to do the actual hanging."

"Got it."

"Same thing in the kitchen. She can watch you cook, offer suggestions, maybe toss a salad, but she shouldn't be standing in front of the stove for an hour cooking."

Ada's cooking skills were somewhere between nonexistent and poor. She wondered if it would be terrible to eat sandwiches the next two months. Probably that wouldn't be best for the *boppli*, plus she wasn't very *gut* at making bread.

"I might need some recipes. I don't have a lot of experience cooking."

"Beth will have plenty, and it will make her feel *gut* to teach you to cook."

"I'm not the best person to put in the kitchen."

"Seems I remember you have trouble cracking an egg."

"Well, *ya*, I do. It's harder than it looks."

They were nearly to Huckleberry Lane when her *dat*'s expression turned quite serious. "This is *gut* of you, Ada, and it's important—very important."

"I know that."

He reached over and patted her hand. "When your *mamm* was pregnant with you, her *schweschder* came to help."

"*Aenti* Mary?"

"The very same."

"I barely remember her."

"When you were four, Mary and her husband Nehemiah moved to Maine. You've read their letters."

"I have, but it's not quite the same as seeing them at dinner once a week."

"Your *mamm* was more tired than usual during that pregnancy. We didn't know it then, but the cancer had already begun."

"I've always felt a bit guilty about that." Ada shook her head when he tried to correct her. "I know in my mind that it wasn't my fault, but sometimes your heart can insist on believing something different."

He nodded as if he understood, then he reached into the bag that he used to carry papers back and forth to the market, and he pulled out an old, simple journal. "I want to give you this."

"What is it?"

"The journal that your *mamm* kept when Mary came to stay with her, when we were waiting for you to be born."

"How…how have I never seen this before?"

Her *dat* smiled widely. "Because it wasn't the right time."

Bethany's house was now in view. It did look small and poor. She'd never noticed before. She hadn't spent much time here. Maybe Sarah and Becca were right. Maybe Ethan was simply embarrassed.

"Over the course of the next two months, maybe you could read it with your *schweschder*."

"*Ya*. Okay. I will."

They'd pulled up in front of the porch. Ada reached over and hugged her father, breathed in the smell of him, thanked *Gotte* for the steadiness of him.

"I have to get home and see to a few chores. Tell your *schweschder* I'll check in on her tomorrow."

"*Ya*, I will."

"And call…if you need anything."

"Right."

"You know the number to my cell phone?"

"I do." Then she smiled and hopped out of the buggy, determined to make the best of her new home. It might be temporary, but as her *dat* had said, what she was doing was important. She slipped the journal into her suitcase and made her way into the house.

Chapter Eleven

Ethan felt as if his life was spiraling out of control. First, there'd been the emergency with Becca and Gideon. That had been frightening and worrisome to be sure. Bethany's emergency had immediately followed that. He wouldn't be forgetting the trail of blood from her room to the couch. He had scrubbed it away before they'd returned home—used a brush and soap and water. In his mind, though, he could still see that trail, still envision the tragedy that it had foreshadowed.

There hadn't been a tragedy though.

He had to keep reminding himself of that. Bethany was home, settled into her room, and Aaron was back—smiling like his old self. Maybe he didn't realize how precarious things still were. Maybe Aaron was in denial.

Ethan had finished storing his clothes in the

mudroom and stacking blankets, a pillow and a set of sheets under the coffee table in the sitting room.

"You don't have to do this." Aaron walked into the room, hands on his hips. "Ada has already said she would be fine sleeping out here."

"No way." Ethan shook his head, wondering what else could possibly go sideways. Now Ada was going to be living in his house. He'd kissed her. He'd thought about courting her, which was bizarre enough given their rocky friendship. With her living in the same house, he threw out all of those ideas.

The next few weeks would be terrible. He was sure of it. Having Ada around twenty-four-seven would probably drive him to the mental facility his *dat* had stayed in more than once. Was this how it had started? Could you become bipolar? Ethan sure felt as if his feelings were seesawing up and down.

"Are you okay?" Aaron asked.

"Sure."

"You don't look sure."

"I could be overthinking things."

"It's going to be fine."

"It's going to be crowded."

"We've been crowded before. What are you really worried about?"

Ethan only shook his head. He wasn't about to

admit to his *bruder* that he had feelings for Ada. Did he have feelings for Ada? He needed to get out of this house. He needed to go to the barn.

So, of course, when he stepped out onto the front porch, Amos was driving up. He couldn't dash over to the barn and hide now. He needed to face up to this situation like an adult.

Ada leaned over and hugged her father, hopped out of the buggy and walked up the steps, carrying one rather small suitcase. Ethan waved at Amos, who waved back then turned the horse and drove back down the lane.

"Where's he off to in such a hurry?"

"Home. Said he had chores to do and that we're to call him if we need anything."

Ada and Ethan stared at each other for a moment, eyes darting away and then back again. Gosh, was every day going to be this awkward? You'd think that they'd just been caught skipping class or holding hands or kissing behind the shed. Just the idea of those things reminded Ethan of the kiss they'd shared—the one thing he was determined not to think about.

"Awfully small suitcase," he said as he took it from her and carried it into the house.

"I wanted to bring animals, too, but my family voted that down."

"Thank goodness."

"What's that supposed to mean?" She turned on him and stepped closer.

Any other woman he knew would ignore comments said under someone's breath. Not Ada Yoder. Ada liked everything out on the table. Fine, he'd give her everything in the open.

He lowered his voice. "What it means is that I think this is a bad idea."

"You were there in the hospital when we all agreed."

"And I spoke up about my reservations."

"Because there isn't enough room?" Ada waved at the couch. "I'm fine in here. I don't need a big bed and..."

"You will not be staying in here. You'll be staying in my room."

"But I don't—"

"I've already cleaned it out."

"Oh. Where will you sleep?"

"Here. On the couch." He waved toward the sheets and pillows he'd stacked on the bottom shelf of the coffee table.

"I'm pretty sure I'd fit on that couch better than you will."

"It's already decided."

"Is that how it's going to be around here? You're going to decide things and let me know later?"

Ethan didn't know whether he wanted to

laugh or sit on the couch and drop his head in his hands. She was so stubborn, so opinionated, so...so Ada. Perhaps he should try to change the subject.

"I need to tell you about your animal rescue meeting." He hadn't been looking forward to this, but she was already put out with him. He had nothing to lose. So he told her that only one person had shown up, who the person was, and what she had suggested. "She wanted me to give you this card."

He fished it out of his pocket and handed it to her.

"No one else showed up?"

"Nein."

She blew out a big breath and scowled at the card. He didn't know what to say to her. Plainly, they all had bigger problems at the moment. So, instead of trying to make her feel better, he said, "Now, if you'll excuse me, I should get out to the barn."

He turned and fled before she could extend the conversation. Was everything going to be an argument with that woman? He made it into the barn and sank onto the old workbench, rubbing his temples. The headache was back—worse than ever. It made him nauseous. He wondered for the hundredth time if he might have a brain tumor. But what were the odds of that? A brain tumor on top of Bethany's and Becca's pregnancy issues? Surely not.

He needed to quit behaving like a child.

There was work to do.

Ethan had never minded working hard. He cleaned out both of the horse stalls, groomed Misty and Dixie—taking the time to check their hooves and comb out their manes. Then he sank back onto the bench and allowed his gaze to travel around the barn.

Needed a new roof, but that would have to wait until spring. There certainly wasn't enough money for that now.

He couldn't do any work in the fields. Since there had been no crop, there was no work to do. There would be, in a few months. But that didn't help him a bit at the moment. He needed to stay out of the house. He needed chores to do that would allow him to avoid Ada.

Standing, he walked around.

Most of the things stored in the barn had been there since he was a boy. His *dat* hadn't been much of one for cleaning up, and since Ethan had moved home, he'd been too busy in the fields.

The fields.

The floods had been a terrible thing to watch. Days and days of rain. Wondering when it would end. Wondering if anything would sprout afterward. It hadn't. Because, once the rains stopped, they hadn't returned. The drought that followed was rare for northern Indiana. The double whammy had left most farmers with no crop at all to harvest.

That was when he'd approached Amos about a job at the market.

That was when his life had been further complicated by Ada. Before he'd begun working at the auction, she'd simply been his sister-in-law and they'd managed to be polite around one another. He could remember feeling friendly toward her—though he never understood the things that she said or the adolescent way she acted. Ada had always seemed to him like an immature young girl. It had been none of his business before, and maybe it wasn't now.

All he had to do was to survive the next two months.

And to do that, he needed to stay busy.

His eye caught on an old blanket covering something in the back corner of the barn. He walked over and pulled off the blanket, which was in tatters. A cloud of dust wafted toward him and he hopped back, giving it time to settle. Then he stepped closer and peered down at what had been covered. He let out a long low whistle. Wait until he showed this to Aaron.

This would work.

This would keep him busy for a while.

* * *

Ada unpacked her things in Ethan's room. It was going to be strange staying in Bethany's house, but she'd just have to make the best of it. She hung up her three dresses, put her stack of books by the bed then set out her hairbrush, hand mirror, extra *kapp* and toothbrush on the top of the dresser. The room was surprisingly clean. She would have at least expected a layer of dust. She moved her now-empty suitcase to the corner of the room, remembered the journal and fetched it from the outside pocket.

She wanted to sit and read it, but she should check on Bethany first.

Ada's *schweschder* was sitting up in bed, surrounded by her knitting supplies.

"Aren't you supposed to be resting?"

Bethany rolled her eyes. "I've done nothing but rest for days. It gets old."

"Uh-huh."

"Thought I'd get started on some Christmas presents."

"*Ya?* It's not even November…"

"Well. When you make things for gifts, you have to plan ahead."

"Hmm."

"Want me to teach you how to knit?"

"We've tried that before. It's always been a disaster."

"True." Bethany smiled and that smile did more to assure Ada she was okay than anything she could have said. "But you're older now."

"I am."

"Probably more patient."

"Probably not."

They both laughed.

"Were you frightened when you went to the hospital?" Ada sank onto the chair beside the bed. "Were you a bundle of teardrops?"

"Bundle of nerves?"

Ada waved away the correction.

"*Ya.* I was very scared when the bleeding started. I… I didn't know what it meant, and I didn't know what I should do." She glanced up, tears causing her eyes to shine. "If it weren't for Aaron and Ethan, I'd probably have just laid on the floor too terrified to move."

Ada tried to imagine what that must have felt like. To be so scared that you couldn't even take a step. To be so afraid that the next thing you did might be the wrong thing…with very big consequences.

"Are you still terrified?"

"*Nein*—not really. The doctor explained it all to me. I know what things to do and what things to avoid. And since we know it's a baby girl…" Her hand flew to her mouth. "Oops," she murmured.

"You know it's a girl? Becca's having a girl too." Then she copied her sister, covering her mouth and saying, "Oops."

"Oh, my. Does *Dat* know? Does Sarah and Eunice know?"

"Not sure about *Dat*, but I suspect Sarah and Eunice know by now."

Wow. Ada was going to have two nieces. Wow!

Somehow knowing that made her job here even more important, or at least it made what they were being so careful about seem even more real.

Bethany fingered the dark green yarn that she had been about to start knitting—probably something for Sarah, who loved dark green.

"*Dat* reminded me of the things you are and aren't supposed to do. Let's see if I've got this right. Do get up and move around occasionally. Do not try hanging laundry or cooking dinner."

Bethany laughed. "You really were listening."

"I was. I'm guessing that also means no scrubbing floors or changing sheets."

"It's going to be a long two months." Bethany sighed heavily. "I'm not so good at doing nothing, but it will be worth it to have this little one delivered safe and sound."

Ada suddenly remembered the journal in her hands. "Hey, Beth. Have you ever seen this before?"

She handed the old journal to her *schweschder*. The cover of the journal was cloth—a dark blue fabric faded in spots. "Look inside the cover."

Lydia Yoder
20~~
Shipshewana, Indiana

"This was *Mamm*'s?"

"It was. *Dat* gave it to me on the drive over here. He said that *Aenti* Mary came to stay with *Mamm* when she was pregnant with me."

"I don't remember that, but then, I was just a babe myself."

"He said that *Mamm* was especially tired when she was pregnant with me, that possibly the cancer had started growing in her, but they didn't even know that she was ill with it. They only knew she was very tired all the time. Mary came to help her. *Dat* said that you and I might want to read through it…"

"This is so special."

"I know! It's like receiving a letter from the past."

Bethany closed the journal and ran her fingertips over the cover. "Will you read it to me?"

"Of course."

"But just one entry."

"Okay."

"We'll make it last. It'll be like…it'll be like *Mamm* is here with us." Bethany looked at Ada and smiled.

This was such a difficult time. Ada didn't want to be away from home. She already missed her animals terribly and she'd only been gone a few hours. Bethany didn't want to be sick. She didn't want there to be any danger to the *boppli* she was carrying. Aaron and Ethan certainly didn't want their lives disrupted this way. They'd had enough problems with the crops. For Ethan, especially, having Ada stay in his home was probably like stealing the whipped cream off the top of his ice cream sundae.

But here they were.

They were all trying to make the best of it.

And now she and Bethany had their *mamm* here with them.

Ada opened the journal and began to read.

"'I am two months away from my due date, and I have been put on bedrest. Bedrest! Imagine that with four littles running around. They are the joy of my days.

Sarah is nine and tries very hard to help her little schweschdern. Becca, at five years old, is already reading and is often content to page through magazines and stare dreamily at the pictures. Eunice is only two,

*toddling about and banging most every-
thing she picks up against the floor or the
wall or the table and then putting it to her
ear. It's as if she's trying to discern the com-
position of things. Sweet Beth just turned
one and doesn't seem to understand why I
can't pick her up. She puts her head on my
lap and sticks her thumb into her mouth,
giving me a woebegone look.*

*I cannot wait to meet the child that I'm
carrying. My heart longs to hold him or her
in my arms as I have held all my children.
Some days I am so frightened that I have
done something wrong, that I have endan-
gered this sweet soul. Amos is my steady
anchor. He assures me that Gotte is with
us still, that Gotte's eye is on this little one
as well our entire family.*

*Now my sister Mary is here. Her pres-
ence is such a blessing to me even though
we are complete opposites and even after
the horrible disagreement we had last year.
And yet she came to be with me, to help with
the girls. I only wish..."'*

"What? She only wishes what?" Bethany's
hands had stilled over her yarn. "Don't stop
there."

"It's the end of the first entry."

"Oh."

"Do you want me to read another?"

"Yes. And no."

Ada closed the journal. She understood exactly what Bethany meant. "I wonder what their disagreement was about."

"I wonder why she thinks they're opposites."

They smiled at one another. Finally, Ada said, "This is the cat's purr for sure…"

"Cat's meow?"

"It's as if the journal has been waiting for us, for just this day and this moment. I can't wait to show it to Sarah and Becca and Eunice." She ran a hand over the cloth-bound book and set it on Bethany's bedside table.

"Uh-uh. Don't put it there. I'll peek."

"Seriously?"

"*Ya.* I have no patience when it comes to such things. Take it into your room."

That caused them both to laugh.

"Guess I should see to dinner."

They both laughed again. Cooking was not something that Ada excelled at.

"Some of the ladies from the church stocked the fridge. All you'll need to do is heat up one of the casseroles."

"I can do that."

"Slice the bread, make a salad…"

"Yikes. Slow down there, Captain Nemo."

"Who?"

But Ada was already walking to her room. She set the journal carefully in a drawer so she wouldn't be tempted, and then returned to see to whatever needed to be done in the kitchen. This stay might not be so bad, after all. If she could crack the apple hiding out in the barn. After all, Ethan couldn't stay there forever. She'd win him over. Everyone said she had a way about her, that she could win over a fence post—whatever that meant.

She had enjoyed the kiss, and she wouldn't mind dating Ethan, but he didn't seem ready for that. He seemed to her like a scared kitten, like the smallest calico from her rescued kittens. He always trembled when you picked him up. Ada had named him Mouse, because he shook like a tiny scared mouse.

Sometimes Ethan reminded her of Mouse.

But what exactly was he afraid of?

She didn't know, couldn't begin to guess. Maybe she didn't have to know. Maybe all she had to do was to offer him the tried-and-true gift of friendship.

And the journal had already given her some ideas for exactly how to do that too.

Chapter Twelve

It was Saturday evening before Ethan had a chance to show Aaron what he'd found in the barn.

After letting out a long, low whistle, Aaron said, "Do you think these were ours?" He ran his fingers along the dusty cherrywood.

"Probably. I can't think why anyone else's crib and child's bed would be out here."

"So, they're old."

"They're antique," Ethan corrected. "Makes them even more valuable."

"We'll have to tell *mamm* when we talk to her tomorrow." It was their habit to walk to the phone booth and call their *mamm* on Sunday evenings. That and the letters they sent back and forth kept them connected. It at least made it seem like they had a family.

"Thought I'd sand it down, then go to the library and do some research on what type of finish is best for babies and then…you know…do that."

"Sounds like a lot of work."

"I don't mind."

Aaron pointed a finger at his brother. "You're saying you don't mind hiding in the barn. What gives? Why are you avoiding Ada?"

"I'm not avoiding her."

"You most definitely are."

"Okay, well, it just so happens that Ada gets on my nerves. You know how she's always saying things wrong, and she's very opinionated. Plus, she can't even cook."

There was the sound of something bouncing against the barn door. Ethan walked back into the main room, but he didn't see anything out of place. He figured the sound must have been the wind. The barn was standing so precariously, he wouldn't be surprised if a good wind knocked it over.

Aaron had followed him out, carrying a section of the crib. "Don't you think that a comment like that is a bit sexist?"

"What are you talking about?"

"Your complaining that Ada doesn't know how to cook. Do you actually think that just because she's a woman she's supposed to know how to cook?"

"Most women do…most Amish women do."

"Not to worry. We won't starve. Our refrigerator is stocked with casseroles, and there are so many desserts Bethany insisted on putting some in the freezer. She said otherwise you and I might start to look like her. Our fellow church members have been very kind."

They finished carrying the parts of the crib into the main room of the barn and stacked them next to the workbench.

"You do know that you can't hide out here for the next two months."

"I can try."

"I don't understand you."

"Trust me, *bruder*, you're better off not understanding."

But Aaron didn't hear him. Aaron was already headed for the door, back toward his wife, back into the house.

Just as well.

He really did not want to confess to his *bruder* that he had feelings for Ada. Did he have feelings for Ada? Good grief. He was acting like a young scholar, hiding out behind the bathrooms during recess because he was too embarrassed to talk to a girl.

He looked through the drawers on his workbench and found a new piece of sandpaper. Cutting it into strips, he went to work on the crib.

He didn't get far though. Moments after Aaron had left the barn, Ada stormed in.

He could tell, even in the low light coming from his work lanterns, that she was boiling mad. Her hands were on her hips, her eyes wide, and her mouth formed one grim line. Even at her angriest, she was beautiful, and that thought didn't comfort him at all. He should be in a duck-and-cover position, not thinking about how beautiful Ada Yoder was when she was angry.

"I've had it with you, Ethan King."

"Excuse me?"

"I've tried to. Believe me, I have tried to excuse you, but you don't make that very easy."

"I don't know what you're talking about, Ada."

He tried to turn his attention back to the crib, but she marched closer, leaned over and spoke in a growl. "I get on your nerves, do I?"

"You are right now."

"I'm always saying things wrong?"

He stood straighter. "Everyone knows that. In fact, I think you do it on purpose to get attention." It was beginning to dawn on him that she'd overheard his conversation with Aaron. That wasn't good. He'd definitely intended for his complaints to stay with his *bruder*. "Were you eavesdropping?"

"I'm opinionated and…" She'd been ticking

items off on her fingers, but now she shook her pointer finger at him. "And I can't cook!"

"You burned a casserole that only needed heating up. How does a person do that?"

"I am so mad at you…" She stomped her foot, actually stomped her foot, which caused him to smile.

He shouldn't have smiled. She might have simply had her say and left if he hadn't smiled. Instead of leaving, though, she glared at him even more intensely and plunked herself down on the workbench.

"Oh, Ethan." She leaned forward, elbows on her knees, and covered her face with her hands.

"Say, it's not that bad."

She didn't look up. Didn't throw another angry look at him or defend herself or misquote a saying. He certainly hoped she wasn't crying. He couldn't think of anything more awkward than having to deal with a crying woman.

"I was just being a grump. You know me, old grumpy Ethan. It's nothing personal."

She peeked at him through her fingers, but she still didn't speak. That was unusual. Ada always had something to say.

"Hey." He sat beside her on the bench—not too close though. No need tempting himself to put an arm around her or to kiss her again. He cleared his throat and tried to focus on the current problem. "Don't pay any mind to the things I say. I'm just... I'm trying to cope, Ada, and I'm not doing a very *gut* job."

She straightened. "You're doing a great job. What are you talking about? You're like the Rock of Gemini."

"Gibraltar?" He raised his eyebrows and waited.

Ada shrugged. "Whatever. My point is that you are doing a great job helping your *bruder* and Bethany, and even their baby. I, on the other hand, can't even reheat a casserole, as you so graciously pointed out."

"I apologize for saying those things." He waited then added, "Do you accept my apology?"

"Okay. But, Ethan...what do I do that gets on your nerves? Why don't you like me? I thought you might like me when you kissed me. And before that even, when we were visiting farms together, you seemed very comfortable around me. Now you're all prickly."

"Maybe because what I was feeling for you scared me." He was surprised that he'd actually said that. He'd thought it...many times...but now he'd said it.

"Oh." Ada glanced at him then jumped up and moved over to the crib. "I guess it is scary, sometimes, having emotions that are...different than what you're used to."

"I guess so."

"But we'll find a way past that. Won't we?"

He'd stood, as well, then he'd stepped closer and now, when she turned his way, she cut the small space between them by half. He took a step back, nearly tripping over a crate in the process.

Ada rolled her eyes and turned to the workbench. "What are you working on?"

"Found this old crib in the corner of the barn. Thought I'd see if I could refinish it for the *boppli*."

"That's a great idea. Can I help?"

The last thing that Ethan wanted was Ada out in the barn helping him every night, but when she turned to him, when she looked at him with those beautiful blue eyes… "I guess I could use some help."

She actually clapped her hands together. "Tomorrow night then. I promised to do the dishes tonight, and trust me…that casserole dish is not going to be easy to clean. It has burned stuff all over it."

"I'll help," he heard himself say. This was becoming an out-of-body experience. There was the Ethan who normally walked around, and the Ethan who chased impossible thoughts inside his head. The two were fighting for dominance.

"Okay. Thanks. I never was that *gut* at cleaning up the kitchen. I guess I'll have to learn though."

"Maybe it's something we can do together at night."

"Ya?"

"Sure. Cleaning and…" He jerked a thumb back toward the barn.

"The crib."

"Uh-huh." Soon he would be simply grunting.

It was like his brain was on freeze. Somehow, some way, he was going to have to learn to be around Ada Yoder. She was here for at least two months. She obviously wasn't the kind of woman to stew over something. She'd overheard him complaining about her and confronted him right away about it. That was sort of commendable. He'd always avoided confrontation. Maybe her way was better.

They closed up the barn and turned toward the little house on Huckleberry Lane. It had been his home all of his life, except for those few years he'd spent learning to be a farmer in Ohio. He loved this place, and he wanted to care for it.

He wanted to see his *bruder*'s family grow up here.

And maybe, just maybe, one day he'd have a family of his own. That day, though, was very far away.

"Hey, Ada…" He waited for her to turn to

him, waited until he was sure he had her complete attention. "I'm not ready to be anything other than *freinden*. Everything is too up in the air right now. I'm worried about Aaron and Bethany and the baby. I'm worried about the farm. I even worry about my job at the auction."

She didn't interrupt, simply tilted her head and waited.

"Plus the fact that we're going to be tripping over each other in this tiny house."

Now a smile once again spread across her face. She tucked a hand through his arm as they walked toward the front porch. "I like your house, Ethan."

"What's there to like?"

"It has good muscles."

"Good bones?"

"It's quaint."

"I'll agree with you there." He stopped at the bottom of the porch steps because he needed to be certain she understood him. He needed to make sure that she was completely clear on what he was offering—friendship and only friendship. "So I won't say any mean things about you. At least, I'll try not to."

"And I won't eavesdrop, though honestly that was an accident."

"But there won't be any more kisses either. We'll keep this on the up-and-up."

"'Up-and-up'?"

"On the level—you know. Nothing like sneaking-in-the-barn kissing."

"Oh."

"We're adults, and we'll act like it."

"Right. Adults. Got it."

They shook hands on the deal. Ethan felt both better and worse at the same time. How was that possible? But as he followed her into the *quaint* house, he was at least grateful they'd talked it over. It would be tough having Ada as a friend and a houseguest, but it would be a whole lot harder to risk putting his heart on the line.

The four of them went to church services together the next day. They were having the meeting outdoors at Bishop Ezekiel's place. Ada had been coming to Ezekiel's farm since she was a child. It felt like the home of a favorite *onkel*.

She sat in the row with her *schweschdern*, where she always sat—except this time Becca and Sarah were missing. Becca was on strict bedrest, and Sarah had stayed home in case Becca needed anything. That meant it was only Eunice, Bethany and Ada. That didn't seem right. She did not like change, and she especially did not like this change.

Ada tried to join the singing. She almost laughed when she heard Ethan and Aaron singing from across the aisle. Ethan had a baritone voice and Aaron's was a little higher. They sounded *gut* together. She wanted to peek over at them, but she forced herself to keep her attention where it was supposed to be—on the Lord and the sermons and the Scripture.

They sang "Precious Memories" and "Victory in Jesus" and "The Love of God"...all her favorites. But Ada had trouble focusing on the words. Why was her family going through such a difficult patch? Two pregnancies at the same time and both of them having trouble? What were the odds?

Why did bad things have to happen?

Had they done something wrong?

Were they in for a long run of bad stuff like Job in the Old Testament had been? Ada did not want her faith tested like that. Job lost his animals, then his servants, then a house collapsed and killed his sons and daughters. He had sores all over his body. His friends were no help, and his wife told him to curse *Gotte* and die.

Ada's life looked pretty *gut* compared to Job's. She was pretty sure she would curl up in a ball and hide if any of those things happened to her.

She helped in the serving line, picked at her food and tried to listen to her *freinden's* cheerful chatter. Her heart wasn't in it though. She finally offered her scraps to Ezekiel's beagle...which made her miss Ginger and Snapp even more.

Deciding she needed a walk, she put her dishes in the sudsy bucket and took off over to the pasture fence. She was standing there, arms folded across the top rung, staring out at the horses grazing in the far corner, when Ezekiel walked up.

"Baxter here looked as if he wanted to join you. I hope you don't mind."

"I don't mind. That's his name? Baxter?"

"Yup. Seemed to fit him, though I couldn't tell you why."

"I love it. I've never known a Baxter." Ada reached down and scratched Baxter's belly when he presented it to her, but it only made her feel better for a moment. Soon, her mind was off and worrying again.

"Do you want to talk about whatever's bothering you?"

"I'm not sure I know how."

"Okay. Let's just walk then."

But as they walked, the things that had been worrying her started spilling out, like water tumbling over a stony brook. The failure of her animal society to attract any members. Ethan's dissatisfaction with her staying in his home. Missing her animals. And, of course, the biggest thing—her fear for Bethany and Becca and their *bopplin*.

When she'd finally finished, Ezekiel nodded and said, "That's a lot of stuff for one person to carry around."

"It is. Makes me tired before I'm half through with the day. Now I know how old people feel."

Ezekiel chuckled.

They didn't speak again until they'd reached an old wooden bench. Ezekiel sat, Baxter rolled in the dirt at his feet, and Ada perched on the edge of the bench. Ezekiel picked up a stick and began scratching in the dirt.

Ada sat straighter.

He was writing letters. F. A. I. T. H. Then using the stick as a pointer, he said, "Forsaking all, I trust Him."

"But I'm not sure I can trust him." Ada slapped her hand over her mouth. "That was sacrilegious. I shouldn't have said that."

"It's never blasphemous to admit what's in your heart, Ada. Our *Gotte* is big. He can handle your doubts."

"My doubts are the problem. How can I trust him when Becca is bedridden and Bethany nearly so?" When he didn't answer, when he didn't try to placate her at all, she added, "Why do bad things happen, Ezekiel?"

"Ah, and there's the crux of the thing."

She was leaning forward, once again petting

Baxter, but she peered up at Ezekiel and caught him smiling.

"So?"

"So what?"

"So what's the answer, Ezekiel?"

He laughed and stood. Baxter immediately jumped up, and Ada did the same. They continued walking along the fence line, though now they were headed back toward the group of friends and family settled around the picnic tables.

"Can't say as I know the answer. It's a question that most of us struggle with from time to time."

"Hmm. I thought you'd know all the answers...you being a bishop and all."

He shook his head and smiled when she put her hand through his arm.

"I don't have all the answers, but I'll pray for you."

"Danki."

"And any time you want to talk, you come and see me and Baxter. We're both *gut* at listening."

Somehow, those words lightened the pressure in Ada's chest. Maybe she didn't need answers. Maybe she just needed friends who were willing to share her burden.

Later that afternoon, she sat next to Bethany's bed. Though Bethany had attended church and seemed to enjoy the service and luncheon, she was plainly quite tired.

"I'll let you sleep," Ada said.

"Nein."

Ada arched her eyebrow and waited.

"Read to me from the journal."

So she went to her room, fetched the journal, and opened it to the next entry.

"'About that argument with Mary. It seems so silly now, but at the time I was quite certain that I was right. I felt sure that I was justified in my anger.

She had visited in the summer last year, as was her habit. Mary has always been what my mamm would call fastidious. Everything is to be done a certain way, and if it's not...if it's not done to her standards, then it has been done badly.

During that visit it seemed that she criticized everything. My cooking. My housekeeping. Even the way I was raising my children. One day—I remember it was a Monday morning because we were doing the laundry—I finally had enough. I told her if she couldn't say something nice, something good or beneficial, then she shouldn't speak. If I had stopped there, it might have been all right, but I didn't. I added the sugges-

tion that perhaps she should leave, go home where everything met her expectations.

She was gone the next morning.

We didn't speak on the phone for six months and our letters were short, stiff, formal things.

Then Dat died—so suddenly and unexpectedly that it felt like a storm from a clear blue sky. He seemed so young to me—only fifty-two. No one even knew that he had a heart condition. One day he was working in the fields. The next we were standing in the cemetery, listening to the bishop read from the third chapter of Ecclesiastes. "To everything there is a season, and a time to every purpose under heaven."

My heart ached for my father, for the loss that had broken my mother, but mostly I hurt for my schweschder. Mary had always been my best friend and I missed her. That evening I apologized, though I could barely get the words out as she kept interrupting with her own apology. Our father's death brought us back together.

Now she is here with me, helping me, comforting me.

Not that she's changed completely—she still tsks when she finds a bed not made with crisp corners or a windowpane with *streaks. But it's followed by a small smile and a kind look. Being particular about things is her nature, but she's softer now. She's more kind than she used to be.*

As for me, maybe I'm learning not to wear my feelings on my shoulders. To appreciate this day. To love those who are with me."'

Ada closed the journal. "How can something that was written so long ago still touch my heart so profoundly?"

"I was thinking the same thing." Bethany reached for her hand and squeezed it. "I'm glad you're here, Ada."

"As am I, *schweschder*." She leaned forward, kissed Bethany's cheek and laid a hand gently on her protruding stomach. "Now it's time for the two of you to rest."

Ada didn't need rest.

She couldn't have napped if she'd been forced to. Instead, she walked outside, thinking of loss and how it changed your perspective. Thinking that, for everything, there was a season.

Chapter Thirteen

The next day Ada and Bethany began preparing for Christmas, though the calendar proclaimed they were still in the last few days of October. Regardless, the crisp fall air reminded Ada of the snow that was to come, and immersing themselves in Christmas was a lot better than worrying about the *boppli* or the finances.

Bethany was frowning at her box of craft supplies. "I usually give Christmas packages to each of the campers staying in the RV park, but I don't see how I can do that this year."

"Maybe you can, with my help. What kinds of things do you give them?"

"Hand-sewn potholders…"

"I'm not very good at sewing."

"Knitted mug cozies…"

"Still can't knit."

Bethany fingered a bit of gold ribbon. "How about cinnamon potpourri? We could make that."

"Is it hard? And what would we need in way of supplies?"

Bethany pulled a pad of paper toward her and started a list. Most of the items they had around the house, but they'd need to ask Aaron or Ethan to pick up oranges, cinnamon sticks and a large bag of cranberries. They spent the rest of the morning cutting out pictures from last year's Christmas cards. The pictures would be glued to the back of each bag, giving it a little bit of stiffness and adding a jolly Christmas touch.

As Amish, they celebrated Christmas in a more subdued way than *Englischers*. They were big on sending Christmas cards. Most years they received fifty or sixty from family and friends in different states. And they had always had one night where they sat around the table and addressed the ones they would send out, eating freshly baked cookies and drinking hot chocolate.

Cards, simple gifts, and the Christmas meal were the highlights of their celebration. And, of course, the school Christmas play.

Few Amish had a Christmas tree in their home. They didn't have electric lights adorning the house. And they didn't go in for Christmas stockings on the hearth. Ada had never missed those things because she'd never had them. No one she knew had them, except for an *Englisch* friend she'd hung around with when she was fifteen.

Thinking of Jocelyn, Ada started laughing.

"What's so funny over there?" Bethany paused in cutting out a Christmas sleigh from a card their cousins in Kentucky had sent.

"I was thinking about Jocelyn McCreary. Do you remember her?"

"Red hair? Freckles? Laughed a lot?"

"That describes Jocelyn perfectly. I was remembering going over to her house before Christmas. Her mother had decorated three Christmas trees." Ada stopped cutting out a photo of a dog in a Santa hat. "One was positioned in the front window of the house, which was actually the study. Another, even larger, tree was in the living room. And then upstairs in the hall was a third."

"I remember you bringing home an inflatable Snoopy that you wanted to put in the front yard."

"He had a red hat and green scarf, and he was perched atop a dog house decorated with lights."

"You thought Eunice could rig up a solar panel to a pump that would inflate the thing."

"She probably could have too."

"Then *Dat* stepped in and gave us all the Christmas lecture."

Both Bethany and Ada smiled at the memory of that. Their *dat* had always made a point of explaining to them why—as Amish—they did things a bit differently. He'd emphasized that the *Englisch* way wasn't wrong, just different, and so Ada had given the inflatable Snoopy to one of the shops in town.

Before lunch, Ada and Bethany took a walk in the cool autumn weather and picked up pine cones and small leaves.

Ada kept a close eye on her *schweschder*, making sure she didn't get too tired and not allowing her to bend to pick up the pine cones.

"I'm not ill, only pregnant," Bethany teased.

"*Ya*, but we'll be careful all the same."

And somehow, walking around the farm with a basket draped over their arms, focusing on doing something for the campers at the market's RV park, focusing on the *wunderbaar* day...all those things conspired to ease the worry that had been plaguing Ada.

That afternoon Eunice stopped by. The three women sat on the porch and Ada again read from their mother's journal—read of how her mother's body grew weaker even as her faith strengthened. Her journal entries shone with the tremendous joy she found in her family, in all of her girls, in writing about some little thing they said or did.

"It's as if she's here with us when you read from that." Eunice drummed her fingers against the arm of the rocker. "I wonder why *Dat* shared it with us now."

"Because he thinks now is when we needed to read it," Bethany said.

"He's not wrong." Ada shrugged. "The billy goat in the room."

"Elephant?" Eunice tossed a look at Bethany, who laughed.

"Whatever. The thing we're all tiptoeing around is that we wish *mamm* was here to help us through this time. *Dat* does the best he can…"

"And he does a *gut* job," Eunice interjected.

"He does, but we miss her."

"We all miss her." Bethany placed both hands on her stomach and sighed, which seemed to express all that needed to be said.

Eunice stayed with Bethany while Ada walked to the phone booth. They had the emergency phone her *dat* had sent with her, but it was for emergencies. He'd made that quite clear before handing it to Ada. So she left it on the counter, where they could find it should the need arise, and walked to the phone booth at the corner of Huckleberry Lane and the county road.

Pulling Sally's card from her pocket, she stared at the message written on the back.

Ada, call me.
I think we can help each other.

* * *

Honestly, she didn't think that statement was true, but it would be impolite to not phone the woman and say so.

"Sally Drummond, SPCA. How can I help you?"

"Um, this is Ada… Ada Yoder. I believe you came to my meeting—well, it wasn't much of a meeting since no one showed except for you and Ethan."

"I remember. I'm so glad you called."

She was? Ada didn't know how to answer that, so she waited.

"Ada, did we meet at the music festival a few weeks ago? I was working the SPCA booth and I think you stopped by and picked up a flyer."

"Oh, *ya*. We did. I had forgotten about that."

"Ethan explained a little about what you're trying to do. I wonder if you could come into town and meet with me. I'd like to speak with you about helping animals in need."

A part of Ada wanted to say no and hang up the phone. This was not the right time to be worrying about the care of animals she didn't even know. When would she possibly find the time? She had plenty to do watching over Bethany and doing house chores that she'd never done before.

But those last four words rang in her mind—

helping animals in need. Those words pricked a tender spot in her heart.

"I suppose I could do that. When would be a *gut* time?"

"How about tomorrow for lunch?"

She thought that Eunice would be willing to come over again, so she said yes.

The next day she met with Sally at Jojo's Pretzels. A pretzel wasn't really lunch, but it hit the spot.

"Here's my idea," Sally said, jumping right into the conversation as soon as they were seated. "I think we could use you on our team."

"Your team?"

"In our office. We don't have any Amish volunteers or workers, and that's a segment of the community that we'd like to offer our services to."

"Volunteers?" She turned her coffee mug this way and that, then took a sip. The whipped cream with orange sprinkles on top looked so festive. They made her smile—for a moment. Then she met Sally's gaze and said, "There's a few kinks in that yarn."

Sally looked confused, but waited.

"I work at the market, technically. Right now, I'm taking time off to help my *schweschder* who is expecting a *boppli.* She can't do things like cook or clean floors because of a complication. Her placenta isn't in the right place."

"She has placenta previa?"

"*Ya*. I think that's the official term."

"And you have another sister who is pregnant too?"

Ada nodded so hard her *kapp* strings nearly bounced into her coffee. "Becca is experiencing dangerously high blood pressure, so she's been put on bedrest."

"Your family is dealing with a lot right now."

"I guess so. But you know what they say. Tough times make you cry...or something like that."

Sally studied her a moment. "I like you, Ada."

"You do?"

"You have a fresh perspective, and it's plain that you care about animals."

"Oh, I do." Ada proceeded to tell her about her menagerie of adopted animals.

"Tell you what. There's something I want you to think about."

"Okay."

"I have a part-time assistant. She's moving in January and I need to replace her. How would you like to take her job?"

Ada squirmed in her seat. "It pays?"

"Yes, it does." Sally told her how much.

Ada sat even straighter. "Money doesn't grow in the cornfield. That would certainly help me buy feed for my animals."

"And you'd be doing what you love."

"I'd have to talk with my *dat* first, since, technically, I still work at the market."

"Definitely." Sally reached across the table and shook her hand. "Call me after you do."

Ada walked out of the Davis Mercantile into a picture-perfect autumn afternoon. She meandered past the stores, not yet ready to get in the buggy and go home.

Had her dream just come true?

Had Sally really offered her a job?

Her thoughts scattered in several directions at once. She finally tried to push those thoughts aside and drove home. She didn't think she'd be able to get a single thing done that afternoon. But she did. She and Bethany worked on the Christmas gifts for the residents of the RV park. It helped to settle her nerves. Focusing on other people helped to bring her own problems, her own decisions, back into perspective.

Ethan had brought home the supplies they'd needed. Ada spent the afternoon cutting out squares of fabric from Bethany's scrap box, and Bethany folded them in two and handstitched up the side. They flipped the fabric right side out, then used starch and a craft iron to make them look crisply pressed. Of course, to use the craft iron, they had to go out to the barn and plug it into the generator. Ada insisted that Bethany wait outside while she went into the barn and made sure the crib was covered up.

"Whatcha hiding in here?" Bethany asked when Ada finally said she could come in.

"Nothing," Ada said. Then, because that was a lie and she was terrible at lying, she added, "It's a surprise."

That seemed to satisfy her *schweschder*.

Her *dat* stopped by later that afternoon. After he'd checked in on Bethany and praised their work on the Christmas gifts, Ada walked with him to his buggy. She stood there, stroking Oreo's nose, and repeated the conversation she'd had with Sally...repeated it almost word for word.

She was a grown woman.

She didn't have to have his permission.

But, oh, how she longed for his blessing. She understood that she'd disappointed him more than once. She hadn't exactly been an ideal employee at any of her jobs. Thinking back on those, she thought she'd been rather childish and self-centered then.

Had she changed? Could a person change that quickly?

Her *dat* broke into her thoughts. "We will miss you at the market, but it seems to me that this is exactly the kind of job you would be well suited for. Not immediately though. You've made a commitment to Bethany. I'd want you to wait until your *schweschder* no longer needs you."

"Of course, *ya*."

He patted her clumsily on the shoulder and said in a soft voice, "My youngest is growing up."

She didn't know about that. Most days she still felt like a child trying to find her way. But this day had been a *gut* day. This day she could believe almost anything was possible.

Ethan felt as if he and Ada had fallen into a kind of rhythm over the next week. It was obvious to him that she still missed her animals, though she went home at least once a week to see them and also to see her *schweschdern*. She admitted to him one night about how much she missed Sarah and Eunice and Becca.

"You sound surprised."

"I am. Sort of. I used to think Sarah was bossy, but now I see that she is just trying to take care of everyone. Becca couldn't wait to get away from home, but now she seems so content there. Though she's already planning a mission trip for next summer."

"Ya?"

"Sarah's quite excited about keeping the baby while Becca and Gideon go to work with MDS."

"What about Eunice? Do you miss her?"

"I do. I hadn't realized how much I enjoyed seeing her new inventions or teasing her about grease on her nose. Eunice, she's amazing."

"It'll take a special man to not be intimidated by her."

"Really?"

Ethan shrugged. "I saw her help an *Englischer* with his car once. I can't imagine how she even knew how to do that."

Most of their conversations were like that now—a simple sharing of what had happened that day or what was on their mind.

Ethan had grown to look forward to the time he spent alone with Ada. She still teased him about being stiff around her, but it felt as if they'd reached some sort of unspoken agreement.

They worked on the crib every night in the barn. Ethan sanded the old wood and Ada cleaned it with linseed oil. It was slow, hard work, but he didn't mind it, and he thought that maybe she was learning to enjoy it too.

Could Ada learn to be happy working at home?

Working on a farm?

Turning something old into something beautiful?

Ada shook a few drops of linseed oil onto her rag and gently rubbed it into the wood of the crib's headboard. "Tell me about the auction today."

"You miss it, do you?"

"Honestly, less than I thought I would. I miss the animals, all right, but there just wasn't that much for me to do. At least here, I'm busy. The days fly by."

"There's a lot of work on a farm."

"It's not just that though." Ada stopped, squinted at the headboard then began working on a different section of the wood. "We never seemed to catch up on work in the schoolhouse, but those days dragged by. I would look up at the clock, sure it would be close to lunchtime, only to find that it was ten in the morning."

Ethan laughed. "I experienced the same thing when I was attending school."

"Well, it's no walk in the field for the teachers. Trust me."

Did she mean walk in the park?

He didn't correct her. What was the point? Plus, they did all walk in the fields more than they walked in the parks. He nearly slapped his own forehead. Ada's misquotes were beginning to make sense to him. That could be an indication he was in real trouble.

"Were the supplies I dropped off what you and Bethany needed?"

"Yup. They were perfect." She stood back now, smiling at the headboard.

"Looks *gut*."

Ada ducked her head, as if to thank him for the compliment. "You did a good job cleaning it up and sanding it."

"And you did a good job making it shine."

Ada flopped onto the milk crate they used as a stool. "I'm going to miss hanging out here after the first of the year."

Stop hanging out here? Did she mean stop hanging out in the barn? Because, even after they were finished with the crib, there would be other things that they could work on. Or did she mean because she'd be moving back to the Yoder farm? He'd been so busy growing accustomed to having her around, that he hadn't really thought about her leaving and going back to her own home.

Ethan felt as if his heart had stopped beating. Impossible. He'd be lying on the barn floor if his heart wasn't beating. "You mean because the *boppli* will be born, but I'm sure Bethany will still need help even after—"

"Doubtful. Bethany is going to be a natural mother, and she always was *gut* at juggling more than one task at a time. I once saw her check in a guest at the RV park and knit at the same time. Didn't even drop a stitch."

"Whatever that means."

"It means she did both well—simultaneously." Ada shook her pretty head. "She won't need me once the doctor releases her."

"You'll still visit though."

"I will! I can't wait to spend time with my new niece—with both of my new nieces."

"I can't believe they're both having girls. And they both know they're having girls."

Ada stood and began putting up her supplies. The first night they'd worked together, she'd left everything on the workbench. When Ethan had reminded her—in the kindest way—that they needed to put away the supplies, she'd said, "Fine. But we'll do this Dutch." That, in Ada terms, meant she'd put up her supplies and he could put up his.

"It's going to be a busy new year, Ethan. With lots of changes! Two new girls in the family, my new job, your new crops, because I'm sure it will rain again. We're already getting light snows so that must mean—"

"What new job?"

She turned from the cubby where she'd placed her things. "What?"

"What new job?"

"I thought I told you. About the job. With Sally."

"Nein."

"Oh." She waved away his concerns. "It doesn't seem real yet, but she offered me a job with the SPCA. Part-time, but it pays okay, and *Dat* has given his approval."

Something in Ethan twisted at that.

He'd been sitting there imagining himself coming home to Ada every night, imagining her working beside him in the barn, and them walking across the fields together. He'd been daydreaming, and the entire time she probably couldn't wait to get away from Huckleberry Lane—away from him and their poor, dilapidated farm—fast enough.

"Sounds like a perfect place for you to work." He tried to sound cheerful but the pretense didn't quite reach his voice.

Ada cocked her head then nodded in agreement. "I think so too."

He turned away, embarrassed. Not that he had anything to be embarrassed about. Ada couldn't have known what he'd been thinking, what he'd been dreaming.

"Think I'll go make some decaf coffee and heat up a piece of that pie. Want some?"

"No. Thanks. I'll…um… I have a little work to do out here still."

She looked around in surprise then shrugged. "Everything looks spic and sparkly. You know, if you want some time alone, you can use your words and say so."

He rubbed at his neck muscles, which felt suddenly incredibly tight. "Fine. I want some time alone."

"Fine."

Now she was scowling at him, but the look in her eyes said he'd hurt her feelings. He should apologize. Instead, he turned and walked into the back room of the barn. Once he'd heard her leave—heard her gently shut the door and walk away—he went back into the main area.

Placing both hands on the workbench, he tried to calm his emotions. It didn't work though. Suddenly, he was overwhelmed with this farm, his job, his brother, Bethany, the baby…it was all too much. His head began to throb on the right side. Always, it started on the right side. Did that mean he had a tumor there? What would Aaron and Bethany do if he were to become desperately ill?

Nein.

It was only a headache.

A blinding, skull-crushing, nausea-inducing, dream-smashing headache.

He'd had worse, or so he told himself.

He would probably have worse again.

And with that cheery thought, he turned out the battery-operated lanterns, closed up the barn and sank onto the bench positioned under the roof overhang. He sat there in the cold, his head throbbing, waiting for every light in the house to go out. When he was reasonably sure that everyone was asleep, he finally trudged across the yard, climbed the steps and collapsed on the living room couch—only to fall into dreams of wandering the fields, looking for something or someone that he simply couldn't find.

Chapter Fourteen

Ada put up with Ethan's moping for exactly one week. She focused on finishing the gifts for the RV guests. She started a few projects for her family. She fetched the box of Christmas decorations, which consisted of battery-operated candles that went in each window, place mats that Bethany had made from a green-and-red paisley fabric, and a white and dark blue knitted blanket that went over the back of the couch. Standing on the other side of the room, it looked like a snowscape with a night sky background.

Her *schweschder* was an amazing crafter.

Her *bruder*-in-law, on the other hand, was being a real pill. He barely spoke, walked around with a scowl etched on his face, and asked them to "please stop" if they sang Christmas carols.

She tried to be patient.

She spoke with Bethany about it, at great

length. Bethany cautioned her to give him time and space.

So she gave him a week and the space from the little house to the in-need-of-repair barn. Thursday evening, when he once again fled from the kitchen after eating very little of his dinner, she decided to confront him.

Why now?

Why could she suddenly not wait a moment longer?

Maybe it was because of what she'd read in her mother's journal that afternoon. Something about the "preciousness of time" and not wanting to "waste a single second."

Ethan had pretty much banned her from helping with the crib. The last time she had tried, he had used his words to say, "I'd rather work alone." That was it. No explanation. No, "Sorry, Ada, I'd love for you to be out here with me but…"

But Ada wasn't one to be put off so easily.

She cleaned up the dinner dishes, stored the leftovers in the fridge, and attempted to work on the knitting project Bethany had helped her begin—washcloths to give for Christmas. They were made from a pretty ivory-colored yarn, and though they were simple and plain, Ada thought that her *schweschdern* would like them. Who didn't love new washcloths?

Alas, the project took a downhill dive. Ada kept losing count of her stitches. What should have been a square-shaped cloth now resembled something narrow at the bottom and inexplicably wide at the top. One row had a hole in the middle of it. How had that happened?

She would have to frog it out.

Was that the word?

Or maybe it was toad. Toad it out? Sounded wrong.

She tossed the project back into her bag, paced the kitchen and stared out the window at the barn.

She'd given Ethan time.

She'd given him space.

Ada didn't have any more patience.

She made sure Bethany was being watched over by Aaron—they were sitting on the couch and he was rubbing her feet—and then she snagged up some of the oatmeal-raisin cookies she'd made and marched over to the barn.

They'd had another light dusting of snow and the wind was blowing from the north. She should have put on her coat, but her anger and frustration seemed to provide a shield against the winter night. At least, it did until she was halfway across the yard.

Yikes, but it was cold.

She jerked open the door to the barn, expecting to find the crib done and Ethan reading a magazine.

But that wasn't what she found at all.

"Ethan. What is it? What's wrong?"

Her anger melted away like snow on a sunny afternoon. She set the cookies on the workbench—a workbench that looked as if it hadn't been used in quite some time. Ethan tried to look up from where he was sitting, tried to give her a weak smile, but even that seemed to cause too much pain. He winced, clutched his head with both hands and stared at the barn floor.

She pulled the extra milk crate over to sit on, positioning it in front of him—sitting knee to knee. "What is it?"

"My head," he mumbled.

"A headache?"

He shook his head, then his shoulders drooped as if even that small motion had caused him great pain.

"Ethan, look at me. Do you need to see a doctor?"

She thought he wouldn't answer her. Ada put her hands on his shoulders and waited for him to look up.

He finally did, misery etched on his face. "It's only a headache."

"Looks much worse than that."

Ethan closed his eyes, pressed the palms of his hands against his temples.

"Talk to me, Ethan. It's plain that you're in pain. How long has this been going on?"

"Comes and goes."

"How long has it been coming and going?"

"Weeks? Months?"

"And the pain…what's it like?"

"Feels as if one of Bethany's knitting needles has been driven through my skull."

"Does all of your head hurt? Both sides?"

"Right. Only the right. Tomorrow it will be the left."

Only the right. Tomorrow it will be the left. Those words confirmed what Ada suspected.

"I'll be back in a jiffy." She ran to the house, relieved to see that Bethany and Aaron had moved to their bedroom. She wasn't sure how she'd explain brewing coffee before bed. She was sure that Ethan was trying to hide his pain from his family and, for the moment, until she knew more, she would honor that need for privacy.

Fifteen long minutes later she was back in the barn with a thermos of the dark brew. He had one lantern turned on and set to its lowest brightness. She found the other and turned it on, as well, bringing it closer to where he sat.

Ethan yelped as if the light caused him physical pain, and maybe it did. She turned the setting to low and placed it a few feet away. Then she poured some of the coffee into the lid of the thermos and pushed it into his hands.

He glanced up at her, winced and shook his head.

"*Ya*, drink it. Trust me."

Probably hoping it would make her go away, he sipped a little.

"All of it."

He sighed, tipped his head back and finished what was in the lid. She waited ten more minutes, not talking, being as quiet as a church squirrel. After ten minutes had passed, she poured another cupful.

"Ada…"

"It will help, and this time I want you to eat one of the oatmeal-raisin cookies too."

Ethan drank the coffee, accepted the cookie, nibbled around the edge of it, then looked at her curiously. "I actually do feel a little better."

"*Wunderbaar.*"

"These cookies aren't oatmeal."

"Oh, *ya*. I forgot and used flour instead."

"And there aren't any raisins."

"We were out, so I substituted chocolate chips."

He smiled, the first smile she'd seen from him in many days, and oh, how that helped to ease the worry in her heart.

"I came out to give you a real talking to, Ethan King."

"Did you now?"

"You've been terrible company lately. No company at all, actually."

He didn't defend himself.

"Have you been having the headaches every night?"

Slowly, as if he didn't want to admit it even to himself, he nodded. "I'm worried. Worried something terrible is wrong with me. Worried I'll be a burden to Aaron and Bethany. Worried I'll be no help to my new niece."

"I think you're having migraines."

"What?" His head jerked up and his eyes met hers for the first time.

In that look, she saw the entirety of his misery. She thought about the fact that he'd been carrying these worries alone. She thought of her mother's journal, her mother's argument with her sister, the bitter sweetness of their reconciliation. She, Ada Yoder, wasn't going to wait for someone to pass from this life to the next before making things right with Ethan. One way or another, they were going to take care of the misunderstanding between them in the next few minutes.

"The teacher I worked with had migraines." She pulled the milk crate she'd been sitting on next to him so their shoulders were touching. She understood that sometimes it was easier to talk about a thing if you could stare across the room instead of into someone else's eyes. "She'd have terrible pain. Usually on one side of her head and then, sometimes, the next day it would be on the other side."

Ethan nodded. "Always starts on the right."

"Caffeine helped a little."

"Oh."

"But eventually she went to the doctor. There's medicine they can give you for this, Ethan."

"I'm not going to the doctor." He didn't sound as if he was arguing. He sounded as if she'd asked the impossible of him.

"Why is that?"

He simply shook his head and reached for another cookie. "Sometimes I get nauseous. Didn't realize how hungry I was. Any of that coffee left?"

"There is. Though I have to warn you, I made it quite strong. You might be up all night."

"I don't think anything could keep me up all night." He rubbed at his eyes. "Can't remember the last time I slept well."

"Eunice is coming over tomorrow."

"Okay."

"I can go with you to the doctor."

"I'm not a child, Ada."

"No, but you are a stubborn man." She couldn't

resist teasing him a little. "You could take me to JoJo's afterward."

"Ah. So this is your attempt to wrangle a date."

"Absolutely. I'm not above wrangling." She bumped her shoulder against his.

"Not sure they can get me in so soon," he finally said.

"We'll call first thing."

It felt so good in that moment, just to be sitting by Ethan. To understand why he'd been avoiding everyone. To be able to do something to alleviate his pain. To stop attempting to hide her feelings.

She slipped her hand into his. "We'll go together."

"I feel rather foolish," Ethan admitted.

They were sitting in the coffee shop adjacent to JoJo's Pretzels the next afternoon. Christmas music played softly over the speakers, though it wasn't yet Thanksgiving. The place had a very festive look to it. A Christmas tableau had been painted on the windows. A decorated tree stood in the corner. Their coffee was topped with whipped cream and red and green sprinkles. And Ada Yoder, looking prettier than any Christmas decoration, sat across from him.

"Because you've been diagnosed with migraines?"

"Because I waited so long to go to the doctor." He shook his head. "As you said, stupid of me."

"I never called you stupid, only stubborn." She reached across and squeezed his hand.

Ethan felt as if a barrier that had existed between them was suddenly gone. Ada seemed to look for reasons to touch his hand, stand close to him, smile at him. Why had he never noticed how kind and caring she was? Of course, he had noticed, and it had only made him love her more.

He loved Ada Yoder.

The truth seemed so obvious.

And he had run from that truth. He had been as afraid of it as he was afraid of seeing a doctor.

"The teacher I worked with told me she'd had migraines since she was a young girl. But yours started recently, *ya*?"

He nodded. Then he remembered her admonition to use his words. "I think they started when Aaron and Bethany told me they were expecting a child. The doctor said that stress can bring them on."

"And the prescription will help?"

"If it doesn't, I'm supposed to call him, and we'll try something else."

"That's *wunderbaar*, Ethan."

He nodded again, but his thoughts were elsewhere. He was still thinking about how beautiful she was. About how much he loved her.

He loved Ada Yoder!

It was like being awakened from a nightmare to find the sun was breaking over a brand-new day. That was it exactly. He felt renewed.

"What are you smiling about?"

"You."

Ada's eyes widened. "Me?"

"*Ya.* I was thinking about how you showed up in the barn with your too—strong coffee…"

"Can coffee be too strong?"

"And your oatmeal-raisin cookies."

She laughed with him at that, then leaned forward and said, "I dropped the bat on that one."

He cocked his head and decided that now was a good time to ask, if there ever was a good time. "Why do you do that?"

"Do what?" She popped another piece of her cinnamon pretzel into her mouth.

"Why do you misquote sayings?"

"I do?" She was trying to suppress a smile, but it was pulling at the corners of her lips.

"You dropped the bat? It's supposed to be you dropped the ball."

Ada shrugged.

"Okay. If you don't want to tell me." And he thought that she wouldn't. That maybe she didn't even know why she did it. But, as usual, Ada surprised him. He understood in that moment that a life with Ada would be a life full of surprises, and that thought made him inexplicably happy.

"Actually, it is intentional." She didn't leave it at that though. She stared across the room at the Christmas tree and her expression became suddenly serious. "You know I was only a babe when my *mamm* died."

"Yes, I know. Sarah's been more of a *mamm* to you than a big *schweschder*."

"Exactly. When I was young…only fourth grade… I came home from school and tried to tell a story about something that had happened that day." She pulled her gaze back to him, as if she needed to confirm that she had his full attention. As if she could only share what she was about to say if it really mattered to him. "I was explaining why I didn't like math. I said *math is for the sheep*."

"For the sheep?"

"Everyone laughed, and then Sarah explained that the correct expression was *for the birds*."

"That's when it started?"

She turned her mug to the left and then the right. "My family was still in mourning, though it had been years since my *mamm* died. *Dat*, he was doing the best he could, but having five girls to raise was plainly overwhelming. I must have been ten, so I guess Sarah was twenty."

Ada sipped the cooling coffee, studying Ethan

over the brim of her cup. "That was the year that Sarah disappeared two days before she was to wed a guy named Adam. She returned the day after the wedding was supposed to take place and acted as if nothing had happened. But I heard her speaking to *Dat* late that night. I heard her say that she couldn't marry, not yet. That she couldn't leave us. That we were her priority."

"Wow."

"Exactly. I didn't know what to do. I could sense this sadness, this heaviness, in our home. But I was only a kid. I couldn't make it better. Then I made everyone laugh at the dinner table describing how I struggled with math, and I realized that I could do that small thing. I could give them joy for a moment."

"And now…"

"Sometimes it's habit. Sometimes I have to work at how to say something wrong. It's not as easy as it sounds."

"You're something else, Ada Yoder."

"Ya?" Her somber expression turned sunny.

"I was wondering…would you like to go on a date with me?"

"Is that what this is? A date?"

"Nein. But if you'd like, we could go on a real date this weekend. Saturday night. How about it?"

Ada sat back and fiddled with her *kapp* strings. He thought for just a moment that perhaps he had misread her, that maybe she didn't feel for him in the same way that he felt for her.

Then she leaned forward and said, "Would you mind picking me up in the buggy? I'm living with my *schweschder* right now."

"Oh, most certainly. I'll drive the buggy right up to the porch steps."

"It's a deal then." Ada popped the last piece of pretzel into her mouth.

Ethan had the irrational urge to lean forward and kiss her lips, which had a sprinkling of cinnamon sugar on them. He didn't, but he would. Maybe Saturday night. Maybe after he'd taken her to dinner, taken her on a proper date. And in that moment his heart filled with hope. The things that had weighed so heavily on him slipped away. Of course, there were still concerns, but there always would be.

He would still worry too much.

Ada would continue to make people smile.

Together, just maybe, they could find a way forward.

He held her hand as they walked out of Davis Mercantile, down the street, pausing to look in the shop windows. There were gifts galore. Some wrapped in bright shiny paper. Others stacked next to a Christmas tree. It seemed that everyone was in the Christmas spirit a little early, and that was fine with Ethan.

He started thinking of what he wanted to give Ada. Then he spied a long wooden plaque that said "Have Yourself A Merry Little Christmas." The words looked as if they'd been penned on with a stencil and an art marker.

"Do you mind if we stop in here?"

"You want to shop?"

"I want to ask the owner a question."

Ada might have suspected that something was up, as she stayed near the front of the store looking at the children's gifts. Ethan spoke with the shop owner, purchased what he needed, and folded down the top of the bag.

Ada grinned at him as they walked back outside.

"What's in the bag?"

"Can't tell you. It's a surprise."

"A surprise for me?"

"Maybe."

She made a playful swipe for the bag. Instead of stepping away, Ethan planted a kiss on her pretty lips. A blush immediately colored her face. "I can't believe you did that." She slipped her hand in his and they resumed walking toward the buggy.

"You can't believe I kissed you?"

"Well, *ya*."

"But I like kissing you."

She shook her head as if she couldn't believe

what she was hearing, but then she stepped closer and said, "This is going to be a *wunderbaar* Christmas."

"It is?"

"We can deck the walls together."

"Deck the halls?"

"Your house doesn't have a hall, technically, but the walls will work just fine."

They arrived back at Huckleberry Lane without Ethan remembering one moment of the drive. He'd been completely focused on the beauty of the day, on the coming Holy season and on the woman at his side.

For once, he'd been focused on the present moment instead of worrying about the past or the future. That was something he thought he could get used to doing.

Chapter Fifteen

The second week in December, Ada went with Bethany to the market's RV park to give away the Christmas bags of potpourri. The guests were thrilled with the gifts and many had baby presents to give to Bethany.

"We miss seeing you here," one grandmother told Bethany. "But we're very happy to know you're taking care of yourself and that precious little one."

Precious little one.

That described Ada's two nieces perfectly. She hadn't met them yet, but she had no doubt that both children were precious.

They left extra gift bags in the office where a young Amish girl was filling in for Bethany. *Filling in* was probably the wrong word, as Ada wasn't exactly sure that Bethany would be returning to work. Still, the beautiful December day didn't seem like the right time to bring that up.

"Tell me about your dates with Ethan. We've barely had time to talk."

"We live together."

"*Ya*, and we're two very busy women planning for Christmas and a new baby." Bethany put her hand on her stomach, which now protruded in front of her as if she were carrying a melon under her dress.

Ada didn't understand how one's stomach could stretch that much. Just the previous day, she'd rubbed lotion into Bethany's stomach, and she had actually seen the baby move. Still a little intimidated by the thought of Bethany carrying another person in her body, she was also fascinated by what was happening to her *schweschder*.

"Let's see. He's taken me to dinner, for a drive to see Christmas lights, and to the tree lighting ceremony."

"Don't forget you're working on the barnyard animals together—for the Christmas market that starts this week." Their father had expanded the Plain & Simple Christmas Market to the two weekends before Christmas. It was becoming quite the Northern Indiana attraction. There would be carolers, a Christmas barnyard, a nativity play and, of course, booths to purchase gift items and food.

"True, but those aren't dates."

"Tomato. Tomahto. Tell me more."

Ada slipped her hand through Bethany's arm. "He held my hand as we walked through the market."

"Nice."

"And he's kissed me...three different times now."

"Whoa." Bethany stopped, pulling Ada back since their arms were still linked. "How did that make you feel?"

"Tingly. Warm. As if I'd find found home, which is silly since I have a home—two actually, yours and *Dat*'s."

They began walking again. Slowly, so that Bethany wouldn't tire. It was no hardship. Ada could have taken the entire afternoon to walk to their parked buggy. Sometime in the past weeks, Bethany had become her best friend.

Maybe it was reading their *mamm*'s journal. Last night they'd read of her having false labor pains, and their *dat* sitting up with her all night as *Aenti* Mary watched over the other children. Maybe Ada and Bethany's friendship had deepened simply because they'd spent so much time together. They'd shared their fears and their dreams as they'd completed daily chores.

"Do you love him?"

Ada didn't even hesitate. "I do."

Bethany stopped, pulled her into as close a

hug as their niece would allow. "I'm so happy for you."

"Hey. I'm not roped up yet."

"Hooked up?"

"Yes. That."

"Give him time, *schweschder*. Give him time."

Ada had no plans to rush Ethan. She was still relieved that he no longer hid in the barn. Twice, he'd had migraines, and both times he'd taken the medication. Though it took about an hour to work, and a shadow of the headache lingered, he'd told her that it was completely bearable now. He had even shared his condition with Aaron and Bethany. They were supportive and concerned, as Ada had known they would be.

That Friday evening was the opening night of the Plain & Simple Christmas Market. Bethany stayed home because her feet were so swollen. Eunice came over to keep her company, claiming, "We have some secret Christmas things to work on anyway."

When Ada had protested that she might just stay home and "be a spider on the wall," both of her *schweschdern* broke out in laughter.

It felt good.

To see that lightness in their faces.

To know that she had made them smile.

"How is Becca?"

"Better," Eunice assured her as Bethany

reached forward to thumb a spot of grease off her cheek. "Big. Uncomfortable. But the doctor is real happy she's made it this far along without going into early labor."

It seemed as if their family was finally on an even keel.

Ada went to the Christmas market that night. She'd decorated each of the barnyard animals with a bit of red and green. Some sported a festive collar around their neck. Others had jingle bells on their halter. The camel wore a wreath of pine boughs decorated with jingle bells. The entire night was filled with the colors and sights and smells of Christmas.

Ethan was working that evening, as he would work every night of the Christmas market. Several times as Ada was rambling around, she would stop and study him, stop and watch. He would look up, scan the crowd, find her and smile. It was as if an invisible tether existed between them, so that they were aware of one another even when there were dozens of shoppers between them. Ada had never experienced anything like that before.

She'd never been in love before.

She sang along with the youngies who made up the group of Christmas carolers—"Angels We Have Heard on High," "Beautiful Star of Bethlehem," the "Christmas Hymn" and many more.

She helped in the snack booth where they sold cotton candy and hot chocolate and popcorn. She even worked at the gift-wrapping table where she was in charge of ribbon and bows.

In short, the evening was perfect.

She'd caught a ride to the market with a friend so that she could return home with Ethan. He seemed in a fine mood, but she still worried a little about his headaches. She cared about him, and she didn't want him to be in pain.

"How's your head feeling?"

"Gut. Danki."

They were sitting in the old buggy that had belonged to Ethan's parents, being pulled by the old mare that had been in his family for many years. Ada had fallen for Misty the first night she'd stayed at Aaron's house. The gray Morgan was twenty-two years old and more a family pet than a working horse. Still, she appeared to enjoy being out in the cold December air, trotting along the road—head high and tail swishing.

Instead of going home, Ethan directed them toward the small public park that was alight with Christmas decorations. It seemed to Ada that everyone and everything was celebrating the sacred day, and that was as it should be. It seemed to Ada that the entire world was feeling the joy in her heart.

"Thought we'd come here so we could have a little privacy."

"*Ya?* We pretty much have the barn to ourselves these days."

Ethan smiled and nodded in agreement, but something in his expression was serious. Ada waited. She was becoming better at waiting. It wasn't a trait that came naturally for her, but in the case of Ethan…well, he was worth the wait.

He pulled into the parking area so that they were facing the twinkly Christmas lights that adorned the walking path and trees, and rimmed the parking area. There were several cars, couples out enjoying the evening, but Ethan had parked in the corner where they could enjoy the festive scene but still have a bit of privacy.

"Would you like to walk?" Ethan asked.

"Honestly, I feel as if I've skated a mile in someone else's skates. A few hours at the market and I'm all done in!"

"Then we'll stay here." Ethan slipped an arm over her shoulders.

They were sitting in the buggy, with Ada scooched up close beside him. Ada loved the intimacy of sitting together like this. She felt as if they were in an igloo—snuggled and warm, and tremendously happy. She liked being close to Ethan. Liked being able to smell the essence of him—soap and hay and the brisk coldness of the evening. Could coldness have a smell? She thought it could. In a good way.

Fresh.

New.

"Ada, I wanted to say something to you, and I don't want you to feel like you have to say anything in return. That's not why I'm doing it."

"Okay."

"You've taught me a lot of things."

"I have?"

"How to smile at life, to face my problems head-on rather than simply hoping they will go away, to laugh."

"I think you already knew those things."

"Maybe. Perhaps I had simply forgotten, or they'd grown rusty from lack of use." He pulled back a little so that he could look at her, removed his gloves and caressed her face with his fingertips. "You've also taught me how to love. I love you, Ada. I love everything about you from your quirky sayings to your passion with animals to the way you care for your family."

"I—"

He didn't let her finish. He pressed a finger to her lips. "Don't say it just because I did."

"From the top of my heart…"

"From the bottom?"

"Nope." Ada shook her head and her *kapp* strings bounced with the forcefulness of it.

"From the top, because when I focus on my feelings, on what I know is good and right and precious...there at the top is my love for you."

He pulled her into his arms then, kissed her and held her and then pressed his forehead to hers. By the time they drove back to Huckleberry Lane, Ada understood that she'd just received the best Christmas gift a person could ever hope for—a true and lasting love.

When they arrived at the little house on Huckleberry Lane, Ethan kissed her once more then said good-night.

"Good night? Where are you going?"

"There's something in the barn that I'm working on."

"It's late."

"Christmas is only a few days away."

He was smiling mischievously. She liked that expression on his face. She liked everything about Ethan King.

Once she'd readied for bed, she snuggled under the handmade quilt and reached for her *mamm*'s journal. She and Bethany had decided to give it to Becca for Christmas. They'd received the comfort of their *mamm*'s words, and they wanted Becca and Eunice and Sarah to have the same.

But this night, she still had the journal. She reached for it, placed a hand on the cover, thought of her *mamm* writing in it even as Ada was waiting to be born. She thought of her *mamm*'s words and her kindness. She was suddenly overwhelmed with gratitude for her family, for Ethan, for a life that was filled with love and joy even when times were hard.

She didn't open the journal. Instead, she turned off her lantern, snuggled down under the covers, and fell asleep humming "Away in a Manger" and remembering Ethan's kiss.

The next morning she fairly popped out of bed. Today was the day! All of the *schweschdern* were getting together to make the *bopplin* announcement cards. She fixed breakfast, cleaning the kitchen as she went. Ethan and Aaron teased her about becoming a real *gut* cook, which was silly because she'd only made oatmeal then set out cranberries, sliced almonds and brown sugar to mix in with it. Still, she had improved since that first casserole she'd burned trying to simply reheat it.

Eunice was waiting for them when they pulled up to the front porch of the Yoder home. "You get bigger every day, sis." She tried to pull Bethany into a hug, which wasn't easy to do. Then she said to Ada, "Go on in. I'll take care of the horse."

Ada walked into the home she'd grown up in and stopped in the threshold to savor the sight and smell of it. Home. She'd missed being here, though now that she thought of it… Bethany's place also felt like home.

Becca was sitting on the couch, and Bethany dropped down beside her. They began comparing swollen ankles and talking about how hard it was to sleep.

"I feel like a beached whale," Bethany admitted.

"Sarah baked all day yesterday." Becca rubbed the top of her stomach. "You'd think she was expecting a crowd."

"Well, actually…" Sarah walked in with a box full of card-making supplies. She set it on the coffee table then smiled, ducked her head, and said, "We might be having a few visitors."

"Oh." Becca glanced at Bethany, who shrugged, as if to say she didn't know a thing about it.

"A few of our *freinden* wanted to come by and bring you things for the *bopplin*."

"Oh, I love a party." Ada clapped her hands. "We best get the yarn rolling on these cards before they get here."

Everyone smiled, the worry lines disappeared from Bethany's face, and Becca said, "It's *gut* to have you home, Ada." Then she reached for Bethany's hand. "It's *gut* to have you both home."

It was Amish custom to make announcement cards to send out after a *boppli* was born. Since they would be having two newborns in the space of a week or so, they decided to send out one announcement for both. By the time Eunice joined them, they had the supplies spread across the coffee table.

Sarah had the best penmanship, so she addressed the envelopes. Ada added the return address and a postage stamp. Eunice used a scrapbooking stamp to put pink footprints across the bottom of each card. Bethany wrote across the top of each card, "The Yoder Family is Growing." Becca drew a line down the middle and wrote on both sides of the line:

Name:
Weight:
Born on:

They would fill in the details after the *bopplin* arrived.

Visitors started arriving before lunch. They brought cloth diapers, disposable diapers, baby bottles, blankets, gently used clothing, pacifiers and baby rattlers, crib sheets, two precious quilts that had been pieced together by the women in their church, and lots of jars of baby food.

"Who knew that a *boppli* would eat this much?" Ada said. "We have everything but the kitchen floor here."

"Kitchen sink," Sarah whispered.

And everyone laughed.

Ada couldn't remember a time when she was happier. She thought of telling her *schweschdern* about her relationship with Ethan, but she didn't want to make the day about her. It was about Bethany and Becca and their sweet *bopplin*.

Ada waited until everyone was cleaning up and Becca had gone to lie down before slipping out to the barn to check on her animals. Ginger and Snap barked in surprised then made a bee-line for her, trying to climb into her lap before she'd even sat down.

Matilda lay beside her with a contented sigh, pressing right up against her. Patches meowed mightily as her two remaining kittens tried to nurse. Ada suspected they were getting too old for that. As for Pogo the goat, he bounced twice, lifted up his pretty head and let out a childlike cry, then charged across the stall and bumped into the puppies in her lap. It felt so good and right to be there, to be with her animals, but Ada realized in that moment that there was one thing missing— Ethan. She enjoyed visiting with her orphaned pets, loved seeing them, but she couldn't wait to get back to the house on Huckleberry Lane.

Ethan felt as if he were walking through a dream. Had Ada actually said she loved him?

Had he really been brave enough to say he loved her? Was he actually going to commit to a relationship with Ada? He'd be more than grateful to have her in his life, but was he willing to put her through the difficulties of his unusual circumstances? Ethan knew that his *bruder* had struggled with this very thing when he had first had feelings for Bethany.

Aaron had been afraid that he might be saddling Bethany with a bipolar husband. He wasn't bipolar, but that had been his biggest fear...that he would tread in his father's footsteps. Aaron and Bethany had gone to the doctor together. They had learned, together, what the symptoms were, what the odds were, and what to do if it were to happen.

They'd wanted to go into marriage with their eyes wide open, fully committed to one another, willing to support one another through the good, the bad and the family genes.

Ethan wasn't afraid of bipolar disease. He was simply afraid of not doing enough, of not being enough, of disappointing those he cared for. Ada didn't abide such talk. Ada was firm in her belief that he was doing the best he could. She consistently told him that his efforts were more than good enough.

The next evening, both Ada and Bethany stayed home. Ethan went to the Christmas market with Aaron. As they walked from the buggy toward the market adorned with greenery, red ribbons and twinkly lights, Ethan caught him up to date on his relationship with Ada.

"I'm proud of you, *bruder*. You stepped out in faith."

"When you feel something as strong as my love for her, it's hard to keep it inside."

Aaron stopped in the middle of the sidewalk and pulled him into a hug. It was all the approval that Ethan needed. He'd tell his *mamm* during their weekly Sunday-afternoon call, and he'd tell Amos as soon as he saw the man outside of work.

The evening flew by.

Guests were obviously enjoying themselves.

A few of the area newspapers had sent camera crews and they were busy interviewing guests and filming Christmas Live spots. The mood was one of celebration. Ethan felt the last of his worries slip away. He enjoyed the evening, his job, the smiles on the faces of strangers and friends alike.

He couldn't remember a single Christmas where he had felt this content, this grateful, and to think it all started with both Bethany and Becca having trouble with their pregnancies.

As they drove home, Ethan felt happier than he ever had.

He could barely wait to get to the house on Huckleberry Lane, to go over the evening's events with Ada, to sit with her in the kitchen and enjoy a hot cup of tea and an evening snack.

But the moment they pulled in front of the house, Ethan knew something was wrong. All of the lights were on. Bethany's overnight bag was sitting on the porch steps and it was then, as they were hurrying to the front door, that he heard the distant blare of an ambulance.

Bethany was on the couch and in obvious pain—her eyes squeezed shut, her breath coming out in short gasps, one hand clutching Ada's, the other pressed atop her stomach.

"What is it?" Aaron was at her side in three long strides. "Is it time? Is the baby coming?"

"Her pains started a few hours ago," Ada said.

Bethany opened her eyes long enough to say to her husband, "You're going to be a *dat*. Pretty soon, I think."

"Her contractions are twelve minutes apart. We called the doctor, who said it's early, but she should come in to the hospital."

"You called the ambulance?"

"*Ya. Dat* too. He'll meet us there. The ambulance—"

There was no need to say more. Red flashing lights filled the living room window as the ambulance pulled up behind the buggy.

Ethan stood near the door, taking this all in. His legs felt like two concrete pillars that couldn't possibly move. Then Aaron said, "Help me get her to the door."

With one *bruder* on each side of Bethany, they helped her toward the door and were met there by two paramedics. In less than a minute, they had loaded Bethany into the back of the ambulance, Aaron had climbed up to sit beside her, and they were gone.

It was so similar to that other night when Ethan had been afraid she might lose the child. It was so different from that night.

The evening was strangely quiet.

Slowly, Ethan became aware of the light, cold northerly breeze in the trees, the soft whinny of a horse, Ada standing beside him. He pulled her into his arms. "It's happening. By this time tomorrow I'll be an *onkel*."

"And I'll be an *aenti*."

"Did you call a driver for us?"

"*Ya*. He'll be here in a few minutes."

"I best unharness the mare."

"I'll go inside and look around for anything Bethany might need."

Ten minutes later, an *Englisch* driver pulled up to the house. Ada was waiting on the porch, but she hurried back into the house, into Bethany's room, and returned with a journal. "It's *Mamm*'s. She might…might want to have it near."

And then they were hurrying down the road toward the hospital. When they arrived, the rest of the family was already there. Including Becca, who looked even bigger than Bethany had. How was that possible? Ethan marveled at what that must feel like then thanked *Gotte* he was a man. He didn't think he was strong enough to be a woman. He knew he wasn't strong enough to endure childbirth.

Ezekiel joined them.

Time slowed then seemed to stop all together.

"Does it always take this long?" Ethan asked.

"Depends," Sarah said. But she looked worried.

Dr. Nguyen entered the waiting room and walked directly to them. She was wearing scrubs, including a mask, which she pulled down when she reached them. "Bethany and baby are fine, but we're going to need to do a C-section."

"Surgery?" Amos's eyes were locked on the doctor.

"Yes. The baby hasn't turned sufficiently. She's trying to come out bottom first, and she seems intent on being born soon. It's better for the baby and the mother if we do it this way."

"*Ya.* Okay. You'll keep us informed?"

"I will." She smiled, gave Amos's arm a reassuring pat, and turned to head back out of the room.

Ethan called after the doctor, "Is my *bruder* doing all right? Does he…does he need us?" Aaron had been in the delivery room with Bethany since they'd arrived.

"He's holding up like a champ," the doctor assured him.

"And he can go into surgery with her?" Sarah asked.

"He sure can. He's gowning up right now."

And then she was gone.

An hour later, they were all crowded around the nursery window. The edges of the window had been decorated with some kind of snow frost. A string of lights was draped across the back wall of the large room. It was as if each little bundle of joy was a special gift born on this day for the people who would love, cherish and care for them.

Ethan stood with Bethany's family and Ezekiel, staring at the tiny baby girl swaddled in a hospital blanket. She had Bethany's brown hair, Aaron's eyes, and a healthy cry. The card taped to the end of the bed read Lydia King.

Ada still held her *mamm*'s journal. Ethan saw her look at it and then back at the infant bearing her grandmother's name. He stepped closer to her and slipped his arm around her waist.

"*Gotte* is *gut*," he whispered.

And all of those gathered at the window responded softly, "All the time."

It was as they were watching the new babe that Becca let out an exclamation of surprise. "Uh-oh. I think my water broke."

"Looks as if my nieces will be sharing a birthday," Sarah said.

Gideon fetched a wheelchair.

Amos went in search of a nurse.

Sarah and Eunice stood on each side of Becca, reminding her to breathe slowly. A nurse arrived with a wheelchair, Gideon at her side, and they trundled Becca off through the double doors.

Ethan turned to Ada. "Your family does everything in a big way. Two babes in one night?"

Ada slipped a hand through his arm. "Just think though. These two girls are destined to grow up to be the closest of friends."

That was how it had been for Ethan. He and Aaron had depended on each other because they'd needed to. These two babies would be bound together by the closeness of their birth and the love of their family.

Chapter Sixteen

Ethan was looking forward to Christmas dinner at Amos's house. He wanted to see all of Ada's family, especially Gideon. He had started thinking of Gideon as an elder *bruder*. It was nice to have someone older than him, someone with more experience whom he could ask advice from. And he needed advice today more than he ever had.

As was their custom, they fasted instead of eating the morning meal, though they all had a cup of strong coffee. Baby Lydia had slept a full four hours without waking everyone the night before. Ethan had never thought he'd be grateful for four hours of uninterrupted sleep. He'd never imagined what it would be like living with an infant.

But he loved his niece more than he would have thought possible. When he was holding her in his arms—and they all took turns holding the babe—he couldn't wrap his mind around what a *wunderbaar* and amazing gift she was. He couldn't stop himself from wondering what his and Ada's babies would look like.

They had their morning devotional at the little house on Huckleberry Lane. The words in Luke seemed especially poignant to Ethan—what with Bethany and Aaron and Baby Lydia sitting on the couch together. Ada had pulled in a chair from the kitchen, and Ethan sat in the reading chair.

He cleared his throat as he stared down at the open Bible. His *dat* had never done this. He'd always been too sick—and Christmas more often than not had found him in the depressive phase of his bipolar disorder. Still, his *mamm* had insisted that the scripture be read, and it had usually fallen to Ethan to read it.

This year was different.

Instead of sadness or worry, this Christmas morning seemed to be bursting with joy.

He began with the first verse in the second chapter of the Gospel of Luke. "'And it came to pass in those days, that there went out a decree from Caesar Augustus...'"

He recited the verses that told of Mary and Joseph's journey to Bethlehem, and he thought of Bethany and Aaron's emergency ride in the ambulance. He remembered following the ambulance to the hospital—Ada sitting beside him in the back of the hired car.

"'And so it was that, while they were there, the days were accomplished that she should be delivered.'"

Ethan glanced up in time to catch Bethany smiling at Aaron.

Ada said, "Don't stop there. I'm on pins and buttons to hear the rest."

Soft laughter filled their circle, and wasn't that a miraculous sound in this house—a place that had once held such heartache and fear. That realization brought a lump to Ethan's throat, and he worried he wouldn't be able to continue. He did though. He swallowed, smiled at Ada, and resumed reading. "'And she brought forth her firstborn son, and wrapped him in swaddling clothes, and laid him in a manger; because there was no room for them in the inn.'"

"Crowded house. Just like ours." Ada clapped her hands together. "I never realized how much we have in common with the Christ child."

"He was born poor, *ya*?" Aaron was nodding thoughtfully. "Ethan and I, we've always looked at poverty as something to be overcome...and indeed I'm grateful to have food in the pantry and no holes in the roof."

They all looked up at the ceiling and then

out the window. Snow fell lightly, covering the porch, the barn and the pastures with a beautiful, unblemished white. Ethan closed the Bible. They prayed together, had another cup of coffee, then each shared their favorite thing about the day.

Ada declared she was looking forward to Sarah's cooking. "I'm hungry enough to eat an aardvark."

Becca said she couldn't wait for the baby girls to be in the same room together.

Aaron claimed to be looking forward to an afternoon nap, and probably he was. Being a new *dat* didn't leave much time for sleeping.

"What about you, Ethan?" Bethany rocked the baby in her arms but kept her eyes on him. "What are you looking forward to the most today?"

"Spending it with my girlfriend, I suppose."

That caused Ada to burst into laughter, Aaron to slap him on the back, and Bethany to smile broadly. They were a family, Ethan suddenly realized. He loved his *mamm* and *dat*. He missed seeing them. But the people in this room at this moment? They were his true family.

Bethany went to her bedroom with the baby. Ethan and Aaron had moved the baby crib into their room while Bethany was at the hospital. She had loved the crib, loved that it had once held Ethan and Aaron, loved that Ada and Ethan had spent so many hours refinishing it. Ethan realized that he might not have found the old crib if he hadn't been hiding in the barn. That thought made him smile.

Ada followed her *schweschder* into Bethany's room.

Ethan and Aaron headed to the barn.

Once they were inside and the door was shut, Aaron turned to him. "You're going to ask her today, *ya*?"

"Oh, boy. Do you think today is the right day? Maybe I should wait…"

They walked over to the workbench.

"*Bruder*, if there's one thing I've learned from the medical emergencies this family has experienced in the last few months…it's don't wait. Eat the piece of pie. Watch the sunset. Tell your girl you love her. Don't wait."

Ethan ran his fingers across what he'd carved for her—Ada's Christmas gift. It was a four-foot-long piece of maple, and he'd spent many nights carving the animals, penning the words, wondering if he could trust his feelings, wondering what he was going to do about them.

"*Ya*. I'll ask her today."

"*Gut!*" Aaron slapped him on the back. "We can start the new year with a plan."

Ethan had once believed in planning, and he understood it had its usefulness. But he also understood that some things couldn't be planned for. Some things arrived in your life unwanted and unexpected. He thought of Ada rescuing the pups, Ada purchasing a goat and then a blind donkey. Ada sneaking a box of kittens into his buggy. Who would have thought that his feelings for her could grow so strong in such a relatively short time?

They arrived at Amos's house for the two o'clock meal. Sarah had outdone herself, and though the family had grown by two, they all still managed to fit around the table.

Sarah, Eunice and Amos.

Becca and Gideon and their new infant, Mary.

Bethany and Aaron and Lydia.

Ada.

How was it that he had the privilege of being a part of this family? And if he asked Ada to marry him, and she said no, would it forever ruin this feeling of unity? He didn't think he could bear that. He and Aaron had spent their entire lives alone. He had no desire to go back to that way of living—of existing.

He tried to focus on the delicious food and the banter going around the table, but he simply couldn't. His palms had begun to sweat and his right leg was jiggling. He heard, and didn't hear, the conversations around him.

It was apparently tradition in the Yoder household for the men to clean up after the Christmas meal. Amos shooed the women out of the room.

"I'll wash," Gideon declared.

"And I'll dry." Aaron picked up a towel and slung it over his shoulder.

Amos said he'd be in charge of storing the leftovers in the refrigerator.

"Guess there's nothing left for me to do," Ethan joked.

"Think again." Gideon tossed a wet dishcloth his way. "Table, counters and stove, please."

Ethan had no problem with the idea of working in the kitchen. He and Aaron had done the dishes…even done some of the cooking when they were growing up. His *mamm* often had her hands full with their *dat*. Kitchen duty was a natural part of his childhood, and even when he and Aaron had lived alone at the house on Huckleberry Lane, they'd done the dishes together.

What was new to Ethan was this feeling of camaraderie, of being a part of a group of men, of being a part of a family. Once again, he wondered if he was willing to risk what he had for what he might have. How did someone make that decision?

It was Amos who stopped the circle of thoughts in his mind. "I was hoping you'd take a walk with me."

"Outside? Now?"

The snow was still coming down, though it wasn't enough to worry about. The drive home would be safe enough.

"Let's go over to the barn." Amos smiled as he walked into the mudroom and donned his hat, scarf and coat.

Gideon and Aaron shared a knowing look.

Ethan lowered his voice and stepped closer to them. "Any words of advice on how to ask... well, you know. You've both done it before."

"This is the hardest part," Gideon admitted.

"Other than actually asking the girl that is."

Gideon and Aaron shared a high-five and Ethan rolled his eyes. "You two are no help at all."

Amos didn't waste any time. When they entered the barn, he walked directly back to what they all thought of as Ada's stall. Eunice had let all of the animals out earlier that morning, but now they were hunkered down—enjoying the comparative warmth of the barn. He stared at the odd assortment of misfits Ada had pulled together—two beagles, a Boer goat, a calico cat and its one remaining kitten—the others had been given away—and of course...the blind donkey.

"Ada, she's easy to love. She always has been—even during those usually troublesome teen years. Ada's heart has always been for others." Amos waved at the animals. "Sometimes that makes for more work, *ya?*"

"I imagine it does."

"And yet it is part of who she is. I, personally, wouldn't want to change that. We can all use a little more of Ada's generous attitude toward life."

Ethan realized with a start that this was the moment. Amos was making it easy for him to ask. He needed to find the words. He needed to assure Amos that he, too, appreciated Ada for who and what she was. That's what he meant to say, but instead, what came out was another confession about his childhood.

"I suppose that Aaron and I grew up having to be the adults in the household. My *dat* wasn't able to, not really. And my *mamm* was often overwhelmed with caring for him. That left me to take care of my *bruder*. It might have…" Why did this feel like a confession? Why did his past always feel like a weight threatening to drag him down? "It might have caused me to be a bit cynical, a bit too careful."

Amos nodded, as if he understood, and maybe he did.

"But Ada…with Ada, I've learned how to smile again. I've learned how to feel joy and how to embrace the present moment. I'm a little stubborn, so it took a while to put down my worrying, but it gets easier each day." He cleared his throat and turned to Amos. "I'd like to marry

Ada. I'd like to have your blessing. I love her, and I think she loves me."

Amos smiled broadly then pulled Ethan into a hug.

Ethan felt in that moment what it would be like to have a father…one who could offer advice and a helping hand. Someone who was willing to listen. Someone who would be there in the years to come to guide him and Ada.

Amos Yoder wouldn't replace Ethan's father. But he might provide a balance that Ethan had always longed for.

Now the only question was whether Ada would say yes.

Christmas at her *dat*'s house was *wunderbaar*, but Ada realized that it felt *gut* to be back in the house on Huckleberry Lane. Bethany declared it a perfect Christmas. They all had a cup of spiced cider and a piece of Sarah's cinnamon cake. The snowfall had increased and now the world outside the window felt blanketed in a pure white blessing.

"We're snug as a pup in a rug," Ada declared.

Bethany smiled at Aaron. Aaron smiled at Ethan, and Ethan smiled at Ada. *Gut.* Everyone was happy.

Baby Lydia lay in the crook of Ethan's arm.

Ada thought she could watch him hold that baby for hours. "You're a natural, *ya*?"

"Natural what?"

"Onkel."

"Oh. I suppose I am."

Suddenly the scent of coffee cake, apple cider and pine boughs was overwhelmed by another scent.

"Whoa." Ethan held the baby up and away from him.

"I believe it's my turn." Aaron gazed at his *doschder* as he took her into his arms. "The smell is terrible for sure, but the smile on her face after she's had a fresh diaper makes up for it."

Lydia stared up at her *dat* and then began to wail.

"We're going. We're going."

Bethany stood and took her cup and saucer to the sink. "It's been a really nice day, but this *mamm* is ready for bed." She squeezed Ethan's hand, kissed Ada's cheek, and headed off to the bedroom where they could hear Aaron humming a tune as he changed Lydia's diaper.

"Are you tired too?" Ethan asked.

"Not so much. Want to play checkers?"

"How about we just sit in the living room? I'll stoke up the fire and you can hum Christmas tunes to me."

That made her laugh. Since when had he liked her humming? She seemed to remember him telling her it was off-key and too loud. That had only been a few weeks ago, but it seemed much longer. They seemed like different people now.

Ada sat on the couch with Ethan—not exactly next to him, more like she was on one end and he was on the other. Should she scoot over beside him? She wasn't sure that he wanted that. Did he want that? Then he slid over, put his arm across the back of the couch and pulled her toward him.

"Are you okay?" she asked.

"Oh, *ya*. Tip-top shape."

"No headaches?"

"Nope."

"And you'll tell me if you start feeling under the snowstorm?"

He grinned broadly and reached for her hand. "I would, and I will."

She snuggled in next to him. "This has been the best Christmas that I can remember."

"Has it now?"

"Yes."

"Even in this crowded old farmhouse?"

"Especially in this crowded old farmhouse. Don't get me wrong. I enjoyed the dinner at my *dat*'s. Exchanging presents was fun. It was nice to all be together again, but this…this feels even better."

And then Ada remembered that she'd be moving out in a week. Bethany wouldn't need her anymore. Baby Lydia was doing fine. It was time. The only problem was that moving back home—it didn't feel like home to her anymore. This place, this small in-need-of-repair house on Huckleberry Lane felt like home. It was where she wanted to live, where she wanted to raise her children, where she wanted to grow old.

"Whatcha thinking about?" Ethan asked.

She sighed and almost tucked away her feelings, but what good had that ever done her? Keeping her worries and fears inside only caused them to become tangled and confusing. Best to get things off her heart when she had the chance, and here was her chance. "I was thinking that I'm not looking forward to moving home."

"You're not?" His voice had grown low and husky.

Should she say it? Should she admit that she wanted to stay here with Beth and Aaron and baby Lydia? That she wanted to stay here with Ethan? Expressing your emotions was one thing, but if she wasn't careful—and she fully understood that sometimes her mouth got ahead of her brain—she'd be proposing to Ethan.

Her heart beat faster and her palms began to sweat.

Should she propose to Ethan?

Could she?

"I loved my Christmas present," he said.

"*Ya?* Beth helped me with the knitting," Ada confessed. "I wanted to add nice lines of pink and orange through the gray, but she insisted that men preferred something more subdued."

"The hat and scarf are perfect." He picked up her hand and kissed it.

She liked that.

She liked it when Ethan kissed her—so there! Ha! She wanted to shout it to the world.

"You might have noticed that I didn't give you a gift."

"Hmm." She tapped a finger against her lips. "Now that you mention it..."

He stood, walked over to the fireplace hearth and opened a small box placed off to one side. She'd dusted that box every time she'd cleaned this room, which had been a lot of times. She'd never looked inside it though. That had seemed like overstepping.

"This box was my *mamm*'s. She'd put family letters in it, and then at night she'd pull them out and we'd read...or reread...them." He pulled out a sheet of paper and sat beside her. It had been folded in thirds, as if it were ready for an envelope. On the outside, he had written in his perfect penmanship a single word. *Ada.*

"You wrote me a letter?"

"Something like that."

"And this is my Christmas present?"

"It is if you want it to be."

"Sounds mysterious." She slowly unfolded the top of the sheet of paper. What she found covering the top third of the paper was a very detailed drawing of Ethan's barn. She could tell it was Ethan's barn because he'd drawn a stick horse out to the side and written above it "Misty."

"Hmm."

"Finish opening it."

Her heart was thumping and her palms were sweating again. She wondered why. After all, it was simply a drawing and, if she were honest, not a very good one. Ethan's penmanship was much better than his drawing ability. She did not point that out. She unfolded the bottom third and then her voice caught in her throat and tears sprang to her eyes.

She ran the tips of her fingers across what he had drawn there, stared at it, started to speak and then stopped. She ran her fingers over it again. Had anything ever looked more beautiful to her? Maybe baby Lydia's face. Or Mary's smile. Maybe Ethan. People were more beautiful than this drawing, but things? There wasn't a single thing in Shipshewana or beyond that could bring her more joy than what he'd drawn there.

She carefully placed the sheet of paper on the coffee table and threw herself into his arms.

"Whoa. Does this mean you like it?"

"I love it." She pulled away from him, leaned forward and studied the drawing again.

Ethan picked up the sheet, sat back, and she relaxed in the circle of his arm.

"We'll expand it this way, on the side that is closest to the backyard. That way you can keep an eye on your animals while you're doing other things."

"I love the sign."

"Already carved it, but I left it in the barn. Didn't think it would fit in the house." Across what she supposed was a piece of wood were the words "Ada's Backyard Barnyard."

Ethan set aside the paper then scooted back enough to be able to look her in the eyes. "Will you marry me, Ada? I love you. I'm lost without you. Somehow you always know what to say to brighten my day. You're caring and *gut* and—"

Ada couldn't wait any longer. She shushed him with a kiss.

He ran a finger up and down her face then again clasped her hand. "You haven't answered me."

"I haven't?"

"*Nein.*"

"My answer is *yes,* Ethan King. Yes, I will

marry you. We'll be as happy as two pears in a pod."

He put his arm around her and once again pulled her close. "Two peas in a pod." He kissed the top of her head.

"But we'll be more than two."

"Indeed."

"Beth and Aaron, baby Lydia, you, me and…" She pulled away, smiled up at him again. "And maybe more *bopplin*."

"I expect so."

"It'll be a full house—a *gut* house."

"I'm already planning the expansion."

Epilogue

They married at the house on Huckleberry Lane.

They would, of course, be living with Bethany and Aaron. By October of the next year, the house had been expanded to add two more bedrooms. The two original bedrooms would serve as a nursery for Bethany and another nursery for Ada, when and if she needed one.

The two new bedrooms were larger, with big picture windows that looked out over the fields ripe with harvest. It had been a *gut* year to be a farmer. Aaron had stopped working at the auction house and farmed full-time. Ada split her time between volunteering with the SPCA and raising her collection of misfit animals, which now included a llama and an emu.

Waiting ten months to marry had been difficult, but Ada was grateful for the time. She'd learned to be at ease with the woman she was becoming, to be confident in herself and to be confident in Ethan's love for her.

The two couples would share their joys and disappointments together.

They would raise their families together.

The four of them—five counting baby Lydia—were a family. A few miles away was the rest of their family—ready to lend an ear, or to provide a helping hand, or to give a hug. Ada knew that change was still happening in the Yoder household. She didn't know who, if anyone, would marry next—Sarah, Eunice or maybe their *dat*? That thought brought a smile to her face. As far as she knew, he'd never dated, but maybe he would...maybe as he saw his *doschdern* embracing their own lives, he'd be ready.

Her nieces were now ten months old. Mary was still crawling, but Lydia was trying to walk. The most she could do at the moment was let go of a piece of furniture, stand there wobbling on her legs with her arms held out wide for balance, and then plop on the ground with a smile.

Everyone clapped.

Everyone always clapped.

And then it was time for Ada and Ethan to sit alone with Ezekiel. One by one, her family kissed her and shook Ethan's hand, then they walked outside to join the guests. The sound of their singing the old hymns provided a background of tradition and community and faith for this important step they were taking.

She and Ethan sat on the couch—the same couch where Ethan had first told her he loved her. She treasured everything about this room and this home and this man sitting beside her.

"Today is a *gut* day, *ya*?" Ezekiel sat in the chair across from them, smiled and then picked up the worn Bible he often carried with him. "You two are stepping into a new phase of your life. Today is a *gut* day, and many days in your future will be the same. Some will be hard, though, and it's important that you know where to look for help."

Ada glanced toward Ethan at the exact same moment that he stole a look at her, and she saw the same answer in his eyes that she had been thinking. They had already been through hard days. They'd clung to each other during those long nights and exhausting weeks, and if necessary, she believed they would again.

"The apostle Paul wrote about this in his letter to the Corinthians, except he called it charity instead of love. Charity suffers long and is kind." He ran his fingers over the cover of the Bible, still not opening it. "There's more in that thirteenth chapter of the book of Corinthians, and I encourage you both to become very familiar with those words and Paul's wisdom. It seems to me that the crux of what you're entering into today is there—to suffer long and to be kind. If we can be kind during the difficult times, surely we can be kind in the *gut* times. *Ya?*"

Ada nodded her head and felt more than saw Ethan do the same.

"Let's pray together."

Ten minutes later, they were outside. As they walked to the front of the group of friends and family, Ada wondered how she'd be able to sit through the sermon. Somehow she managed, though her mind did wander occasionally to the guests, the weather, even her new pumpkin-colored dress—the new dress she had foregone so that she could adopt the beagle puppies. That seemed like a million years ago.

Finally, it was time for them to stand with Ezekiel and repeat their vows. Ada was both there and not there. Her heart was keenly aware of how handsome Ethan looked, his tender expression, her family sitting only a few feet away, her neighbors and friends, and even her menagerie of animals. Her heart noted and treasured all of these things.

But a part of her mind was thinking about how she had ended up here. Becca and Bethany's difficult pregnancies had been blessings hidden under wrapping paper. The thing with a gift was, you never knew what was inside until you opened it. Ada hadn't known that she would fall in love with Ethan. She might have never acknowledged her true feelings for him if it hadn't been for the fact that she'd had to face him each morning and each evening. She hadn't been able to run away from her feelings as she had been in the habit of doing.

She suddenly realized that Ezekiel was looking at her expectantly and Ethan had already said yes. What was it he'd asked? Something about sickness...

"*Ya*, for sure and certain, even if Aaron's as sick as a goat, I'll be there for him."

That caused everyone to laugh.

Ada loved that sound.

Ezekiel placed his hand on top of theirs. He gave their hands a warm squeeze that felt like a hug then gently turned them to face their friends and family. "All assembled here, including myself, wish for you the blessing and mercy of *Gotte*. Go forth in the Lord's name. You are now man and wife."

The next few moments were a blur. Sarah was wiping away tears, and her *dat* was blinking rapidly. Becca was trying to catch Mary, who had taken off at a fast crawl toward the house. Bethany was holding Lydia, who was adamantly demanding, "Down." Eunice and Gideon and Aaron were laughing at something.

Ginger and Snap began to bay. Matilda reached over and pulled one of the flowers off the table nearest her. Pogo jumped on top of one of the chairs and attempted to tug a woman's purse out of her hands. Patches, the calico cat, sat grooming herself in a shaft of morning sunlight, determined to look bored with the entire proceeding, but then the cat glanced up at Ada and blinked solemnly. Oh, the wisdom of a cat…

Ada stepped closer to Ethan. As friends and family congratulated them, she kept her hand in his. She wasn't sure what the life in front of them held in store, but she was sure that with Ethan, she'd be ready to greet it. They'd tied the shoestrings and now they were ready for anything.

* * * * *

Dear Reader,

Sometimes the things we are passionate about can lead us to the people who love us the most.

Ada Yoder loves animals. She wants to take every animal she sees home. She wants to rescue them. She's a bit young and naïve, but her heart is in the right place. When she takes a job in the Amish Market's auction barn, it puts her on a collision course with Ethan King. Ethan's one goal is to provide for his family, for his brother's family, and he's not going to let Ada stand in the way of that.

There is one thing that these two very different people have in common. They care about their family, and it's through that lens of love that they discover they also care for one another.

I hope you enjoyed reading An Unusual Amish Winter Match. I welcome comments and letters at vannettachapman@gmail.com.

May we continue "Giving thanks always for all things unto God the Father in the name of our Lord Jesus Christ" (Ephesians 5:20).

Blessings,
Vannetta

COMING NEXT MONTH FROM
Love Inspired

THE AMISH MIDWIFE'S BARGAIN
by Patrice Lewis
After a tragic loss, midwife Miriam Kemp returns to her Amish roots and vows to leave her nursing life behind—until she accidentally hits Aaron Lapp with her car. Determined to make amends, she offers to help the reclusive Amish bachelor with his farm. Working together could open the door to healing... *and* love.

THE AMISH CHRISTMAS PROMISE
by Amy Lillard
Samuel Byler made a promise to take care of his late twin's family. He returns to his Amish community to honor that oath and marry Mattie Byler—only she wants nothing to do with him. But as Samuel proves he's a changed man, can obligation turn to love this Christmas?

HER CHRISTMAS HEALING
K-9 Companions • by Mindy Obenhaus
Shaken after an attack, Jillian McKenna hopes that moving to Hope Crossing, Texas, will help her find peace...and create a home for her baby-to-be. But her next-door neighbor, veterinarian Gabriel Vaughn, and his gentlehearted support dog might be the Christmas surprise Jillian's not expecting...

A WEDDING DATE FOR CHRISTMAS
by Kate Keedwell
Going to a Christmas Eve wedding solo is the last thing high school rivals Elizabeth Brennan and Mark Hayes want—especially when it's their exes tying the knot. The solution? They could pretend to date. After all, they've got nothing to lose...except maybe their hearts.

A FAMILY FOR THE ORPHANS
by Heidi Main
Following the death of their friends, Trisha Campbell comes to Serenity, Texas, to help cowboy Walker McCaw with the struggling farm and three children left in Walker's care. Now they have only the summer to try to turn things around for everyone—or risk losing the farm *and* each other.

THE COWGIRL'S LAST RODEO
by Tabitha Bouldin
Callie Wade's rodeo dreams are suspended when her horse suddenly goes blind. Their only chance to compete again lies with Callie's ex—horse trainer Brody Jacobs—who still hasn't forgotten how she broke his heart. Can working together help them see their way to the winner's circle...and a second chance?

LICNM1023